DRAGON FOUND

DRAGON THIEF BOOK TWO

LISA MANIFOLD

OCEAN TOP PRESS

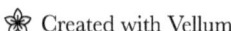 Created with Vellum

To my favorite Dragons - and all our frogs.
Thank you for keeping me going.

LAGNIAPPE

(That means a little something extra!)
Want to meet Aodan before he exploded into a dragon? Click the image below!
If you cannot click the link, please visit:

https://dl.bookfunnel.com/lw4j12jbcv

PROLOGUE

*H*e took a breath, and then another. He was so tired. So very tired. But this had to be done.

Moving carefully, he shifted more of the parchment into the ever-growing pile. These could not be left into the hands of others. If the other fae—if the Fae King, or worse, his mages—discovered his true nature, discovered the truth—they would all die. And it would not be gentle.

At the thought of his children and his grandchildren being put to death, he could feel his heartbeat speed up. Not after all his work. After all the time it had taken to find the others like him. He would protect them all, even after he was gone.

The truth of their origins must never be found, or it would be exposed, and it would be used against them. He shook his head, thinking of the arguments he'd had with his late wife on the matter. She had been for honesty, and openness.

But that was not how things worked with kings. And the Fae King had the power of life and death over them all, every living thing in the Realms he commanded. It was through his skill alone that he'd been given this Realm, allowed to "bring his people into the open."

He smiled without humor. If the mages ever discovered what he'd done, or how he'd brought "his people" into being, it would be the end of them all.

And he would not let that happen. Better there be confusion, and a lack of true understanding as to their origins than to be enslaved or dead.

The dragons would be equal with everyone in this Realm, in all the Realms. He coughed. Which meant he needed to finish sorting these papers. A gleam on the edge of the table caught his eye. Yes, that would need to be addressed as well. But how? Where?

He must hide this where none but his dragon children would find it, but not so well that it would never be found.

There wasn't much time.

1
___

*A*ll I wanted was a peaceful life. One where I didn't have to worry about my next meal, or whether my lights would come on that night, or when someone would try to kill me next.

So, I became a thief. And I'm a good—no, a great—thief. I built, with my best friend Margrite, a decent life. Not great, but decent.

Until about two weeks ago. That was the night I did a job that paid me so well it would set me and Margrite up for life. It would allow us to do all the things we planned, forever. I remember checking my bank account after we got paid and thinking it was all coming up roses for us.

Of course, I woke up that night to my best friend screaming at me. Because I was a dragon.

What followed, in a nutshell, is that I discovered I'm a dragon shifter. I have a grandfather, something I wasn't aware of for most of my life. He's a dragon shifter too. I'm not just a dragon, I'm also part fae.

And please don't confuse that with the tiny hot girls that fly around with wings. It's the fae, not fairies.

My mother, who was human, but fell in love with a fae dragon shifter, hid me from all the dragon/fae/non-human types in the family, essentially anyone who lives in the Dragon Realm. Yeah. There's a whole other world out there. We're here in the Human Realm, and the part of my family still alive on my dad's side lives in the Dragon Realm.

All this is well and good, but it doesn't really do a thing to help me. I knew none of this until the last job that I did, the one that paid me fat bank, was for an object from the Dragon Realm. And it basically turned on the light switch on my dragon side. Totally great timing.

I tried to resist getting roped into whatever plans Fangorn— that's my grandfather—wanted me to do. But then this guy named Eilor, who is the ex-Dragon King, came after Margrite because he wants me. Eilor's not a dragon, but he ruled the Dragon Realm, and he wants it back.

Or rather, he wants my fae/human/dragon blood. Which will help him get it back, I guess? I don't understand the whole blood thing. It's pretty gross, when you think about it. But Aine —my twin sister, who thought I was dead as she was growing up in the Dragon Realm—says that as crazy as you think Eilor is, you're not going far enough down the crazy path. I'm a little fuzzy on the details of his evil plans. Suffice to say I think he's crazy, but he's determined crazy, and that's the most dangerous kind of crazy.

He kidnapped Margrite as a way to make me turn myself over to him. Dragons have a way of talking via their minds, and this guy Eilor learned how to eavesdrop on that. He found his way into my conversations with Fangorn, and at first, I thought they were the same guy. When Eilor realized how important Margrite was to me, he snatched her up and told me the only way to keep her alive was to give myself up to him.

If the Dragon Realm didn't kill her first.

The other Realms aren't friendly to humans. Humans go there, and most of them die. Well, not all humans—I stopped myself. There was no need to fall down that rabbit hole. The humans were an entirely different subject in the Realms. The Dragon Realm, part of the Fae Realm, was complex. And most humans couldn't survive there.

So not only does this Eilor asshole threaten my best friend, he takes her somewhere that she could die even if he didn't do anything to her. Thankfully, when I went back to the Dragon Realm with Fangorn and met my dragon family—another thing too complex to get into at the moment—we worked together and Margrite was sent home to the Human Realm.

She'd whispered the word 'pancakes' when I saw her last. That one word told me where to meet her. But when I'd gone there, looking for her in the small outbuilding behind our favorite place to get breakfast, she wasn't there.

Only a scrap of paper that said 'Peaches.' I knew where to go. We had, after basically living on the streets for the past five years, a code of being able to find one another if we got split up, or it wasn't safe to be in our apartment. Our former apartment, now. Thinking about it still gave me a pang of loss. It was one of the first things that had ever truly been mine. We'd left the apartment, and the entire building where our hideout was located when the muscle from my rival showed up and tried to burn the place down. It had been no-tell motels ever since.

It had been a rather shitty two weeks, overall. Outside of finding I had all this family, dragon and non-human family, and that came with some pretty heavy strings. It brought me to where I was now, where the word 'Peaches' sent me. It meant that she'd meet me at a bookstore called The Book Nook. We'd found it by accident when we were looking for somewhere to eat after a job.

A couple of years ago, Margrite and I had been in the bookstore. I was researching something how-to related. When I went looking for Margrite, she was curled into a leather lounge chair absorbed in a paperback.

She didn't hear me approaching. I moved quietly, looking at

the cover of the book as I did so. It had a woman in a flowing dress looking kind of dramatic. Completely out of any world that I was familiar with. Before she knew it, I snatched the book from her, turning it so I could look at the pages.

"Peaches?" I asked, lowering the book to look at her. "You're reading a book where the author calls you 'Peaches'?" I asked, laughing.

Margrite uncurled herself and snatched it right back. "Just because I don't want to always be in the right here, right now, dirty world we live in isn't a bad thing, Aodan!"

She was right, but that didn't stop me from teasing her about it. Gradually, Peaches had morphed into one of our code words. That's why I knew exactly where to go.

Since she wasn't at the shed—which was the agreed-upon place she'd indicated with the last thing she'd said to me, I knew something had gone wrong. The question was just how wrong? Normally, I wouldn't think anything of it, but this had been a crazy week, to put it mildly.

There hadn't been anything in the shed that indicated she'd been forced out of here. I looked at the note again. There was nothing that suggested she'd been hurt, or in a hurry. Just that she'd felt she had to leave. It was vague, and I hated vague.

I sighed. It *was* a crazy week. Everything we'd had planned had gone seriously sideways. And that was putting it mildly.

I thought about the job that started all this. How could an ordinary box with some nice decoration have such an effect on so many people? Had I known it, I wouldn't have taken the job.

That thought made me pause. Was I really sorry I'd taken this job? I'd learned a lot about my parents. My coat, I thought as I pulled the collar up toward my face. It had been my dad's, and it was dragon hide. Fangorn, my grandfather, told me the coat would protect its wearer.

He hadn't mentioned how, but protection was a good thing, right?

I only hoped that I wouldn't need it. I'd stolen the box, done the job, and dealt with the fall out.

I hurried. It was late—I passed a bank sign that informed me it was 7:43 pm. I didn't know how late the store was open, but I didn't want to miss her if this is where she was.

Rounding the last corner, I sighed as I saw the lit sign for the store. But then I also saw an employee turning the lock on the front door.

Well, hell.

I pulled myself up from the hurried pace and retreated into the shadows between two dark storefronts across the street. Was she still there? Had she slipped out the back? The dragon within me rumbled, ready to get out, be free, fight for what was ours.

There was a movement in the store and the same employee approached the door again. Behind him was Margrite.

I breathed a sigh of relief. She was all right. I didn't want to admit how worried I'd been when I saw Eilor basically dump her on the ground when he'd brought her back through the portal. But he hadn't. One small point in his favor. My dragon rumbled again, but I could feel him fading into the background.

Back to Eilor. Even though he'd sent Margrite back, it wouldn't help him when it came time to kill him. But as Iris (Iris being my…uh…sister-in-law? Part human, part fae, married to the Goblin King. Yeah. The week had definitely been crazy.) had said, I would probably have to get in line. There were a lot of people who were mad at Eilor and wanted his ass.

In the short time I'd known him, I could see why. He was a creep and went out of his way to hurt other people. I'd known people like that, and if something happened to them during daily business, no one was really upset. They'd earned it. Karma was sometimes a terribly beautiful thing.

Everyone I'd met—the dragons, Fangorn, all the fae—they all hated him. With the dragons, it was a loathing on a level I'd never experienced before.

That was one of the things I found intimidating about them.

They didn't look old. They all looked fresh and had smooth scales and no one was white, or hobbled, or anything like that— but they were old.

And they remembered everything. Dragons share a consciousness. So, if something happened to me, I could let them see it—oh, shit. I wasn't sure I wanted them along for the ride at the moment. I made myself close off the door I imagined in my head. I'd discovered it before when Fangorn and Eilor were evil twin crazy person voices in my head, before I knew the truth. Shut them behind a door, and they can yak yak yak all they want. I won't need to listen. More importantly, they can't eavesdrop on what's going on with me.

A wave of something I couldn't identify washed over me as I thought about the dragons. Your family, Fangorn had called them. Even though none of them other than Fangorn were directly related, we were it. There were no more dragons. So, family it was. My dragon woke up once more. He wanted to be free, to fly, to stretch out in the evening. It was a perfect evening.

No! I thought. *Not right now.* I could feel him sink down again.

I'd felt better being with the dragons, even with all the worry over Margrite, than I had in any other time in my life. It felt like that was where I was supposed to be. I wanted to be with the dragons all the time.

But I couldn't. Because Margrite was my family, and she couldn't be in any of the Realms. The Fae Realm, made up of a bunch of Realms, was deadly to humans. Iris was human, but she was also like me. Part fae. Margrite wasn't part anything. She was all human, and she'd looked pretty dire when Eilor had finally sent her back here.

I'd have to be good with just visiting. And making sure that they didn't get to eavesdrop on things I preferred to keep to myself. Like whether—I stopped myself. That was something I needed the door closed for.

Forcing myself to the here and now, I focused on Margrite. I needed to see if my suspicions about her were correct. I'd know soon enough.

Margrite walked out of the store as the employee closed the door behind her and locked it. I took a couple of steps forward, moving out of the shadows so she could see me. I didn't want to make any noise. My heart beat faster. Getting to Margrite, getting her home safely—there'd been no other goal for me ever since Eilor took her and ran back to the Dragon Realm. Now she stood one hundred feet from me. The smells of the dark alley wafted out, making my nose scrunch up. I could feel my heart beat faster. The alley smelled of danger.

That's another thing that's different—I have dragon smell. And it's strong. Like, there was a lot that had gone on in that alley I didn't want to think about.

As I watched, she gave a small nod, and turned to her right. I stepped back and moved in the same direction. We walked parallel on either side of the street for two blocks and then she crossed the street, moving quickly into the shadows with me.

She gave me a hard, fast hug and stood back. "Are you all right?"

"Yeah, are you?" My heart still hung out in my throat, beating wildly. Finally, my best friend was safe.

Margrite sighed. "I don't know."

"Why peaches?"

Without a word we started walking again. "I got there, and when I went into the diner, I saw a bunch of guys who work with Caleb. I heard them mention Stefan. What the hell were they doing way out there? That's not part of their normal area to harass and bother."

I nodded, even though I knew she couldn't see me. "Did you hear anything else?"

"No. It was right after I'd—well, after he—right after I came back." She stopped, and looked up at me before looking down. "I wasn't up to my normal self."

It was a huge relief to know that Margrite was still Margrite.

Even though I could see that she was rattled, and I knew we'd need to talk about it, she was still her. He hadn't broken her.

I put my arm around her as we walked. "I'm glad you're relatively all right. That he didn't—"

She stopped me. "No, he didn't. He scared the living hell out of me. I'm not going to pretend he didn't. But with everything," she waved a hand, "I thought I should get out of the diner and attract no more attention."

"That was a good thought."

"Yeah, I think so." She frowned. "They came out to the shed, and that's why I ended up in the hiding place. I could hear them—they even came in. It scared me."

"What were they looking for?"

"You," Margrite looked at me. "They wanted you. But they said if they found me, they could find you. I waited for them to leave and moved on. Not like any of those meatballs read."

"That's a little rude," I teased. "But why do you think they were out there looking around for me? That's kind of weird."

"Okay, reading is not their strong point. But they can follow orders, and I guess someone knows we hang out here."

I laughed, the relief allowing me to relax for the first time in days. "I'd have to agree it's not a strong point. I don't like that they came there, right when you came back from…over there, but we won't be using that place anymore. Where are we going, by the way?"

Margrite sighed. "Any chance you have our stuff from the last motel?"

"I'll have you know I stowed it safely away and everything!"

"Well, that's a miracle," she sniffed.

Organization of the stuff was normally her thing.

"It's going to take us a while," I said.

"God, where's your bike? I'm a little tired."

"Yeah, me too. How about we stop and get a toothbrush and deal with the other stuff tomorrow?"

"I guess. But I would like you to know that I'm lodging a formal complaint. Service sucks around here."

"I'm so glad you're back," I said.

"That makes two of us. And I'm glad you're back. You have to tell me everything," she added.

I hugged her again. Where to start? How to even tell her everything? There was so much—too much. And I couldn't tell her how I felt when I was with the dragons. It would hurt her feelings.

"That may take a while," I said. "Let's get a toothbrush so you don't take me out tomorrow morning."

She looked at me and then started to laugh.

"What?"

"You're giving me hell about morning dragon breath?" She burst into laughter again.

"Oh, ha ha. Real funny, jerk."

I rolled my eyes and ignored her. Margrite giggled when we were in the drugstore. Then again when we checked into the motel.

When the door closed behind us, I said, "Good thing we have money. All we've done is live out of ratty motels."

"Better than having the building fall on us," she said.

I nodded. Margrite spoke the truth. I felt the pang again at the fact we'd never be able to go back to the apartment. Not like I'm a building inspector or anything. But when a building makes noise, shifts, settles, hums in the wind—it's not safe. That's kind of a no-brainer. Not to mention the fact that our hiding place had been discovered. Since then, we'd been hiding in no-tell motels, the worst kind of dives.

I shrugged out of my coat and lay back on the bed. Margrite headed for the bathroom and I could hear water running.

I closed my eyes. For the first time since Eilor took Margrite, I allowed myself to relax. My muscles sank slowly and carefully into the bed. She was safe. I was safe.

For the moment. I closed my eyes.

2

I almost had it. I stretched my arm out, reaching for the glowing light. I didn't know what it was, but I wanted it. Wanted it so bad I could taste it.

As I watched, my hand, stretched so taut that the muscles in my fingers stood out, shifted. It went from my hand and my arm in my dad's red leather coat to my deep blue dragon-scaled arm, complete with long claws.

"Got you," I muttered, feeling the round shape curl into my claw.

The light grew so bright that I wanted to shield my eyes. But I couldn't. I was stretched all the way out over this—cliff? Edge? And my other claw was holding onto the edge of wherever I was for dear life. There was no way to get away from the light, which kept growing larger and brighter.

Oh, shit. Oh, no. No no no no no! I felt my claw that was holding on start to slip and carefully, my claws scrabbled for purchase.

I almost had it. I was going to be safe.

As I fell from the edge, the round, glowing crystal dropped from my claw, which became a hand again. The wind rushed around me as I fell. This was it. I'd failed. The crystal was lost. Very shortly, I'd be dead. There was nothing but death ever again. The sadness I felt about not getting the crystal was even more overwhelming than the fact that I was falling to my death.

I sat up in bed, sweating. "Holy shit," I muttered. Wherever I'd been, I wasn't there anymore. This was the motel that Margrite and I were hiding out in.

It was just a dream, I told myself. No matter how real it felt. And it felt real. I could still feel my claws scrabbling for something to hold on to, and I shuddered. It was the most real dream I'd ever had. Even more than the ones I used to have about Dani, my favorite waitress at one of the dive bars we used to go to. And those had been vivid. Very vivid.

Margrite stirred in the other bed. "What's wrong?" She asked, her voice low and sleepy.

"It's nothing. Go back to sleep." I slid out of bed, heading for the bathroom.

She mumbled something and shifted around. Then she was quiet.

Closing the bathroom door, I turned on the light and looked at myself in the mirror. My face was haggard, like worry had taken up permanent residence there.

Which it had.

I thought, when I'd come back from the Dragon Realm that all I'd need to do was find Margrite and everything would be fine.

As if. I never had that sort of luck anymore. She was safe, and I was dreaming of failing and dying all in the same dream. Splashing some water on my face, I cupped my hands and took a drink. It was still dark outside, which meant it wasn't time for me to even think about being up.

A last glance in the mirror told me the water hadn't helped much, but maybe I'd be able to get some sleep. I got back into bed and pulled the blanket up, closing my eyes.

The next morning, both of us slept longer than normal.

Usually we got up with the sun. Not this morning. It was nearly ten when I rolled over and looked at the clock.

I threw a pillow to the other bed. "Hey, let's get up. I'm hungry."

She stirred and mumbled something.

Now awake, I got up and went for the shower, throwing the second pillow at her. "Get up. I'm not missing breakfast because you're lazy!"

I shut the bathroom door quick. A moment later, I heard a thump. Peeking out, there was a pillow lying next to the door.

"Hurry up," Margrite sat up, dark hair sticking up around her head, eyes glaring.

I laughed as I shut the door again. Despite my laughter, I felt edgy and unsettled. Margrite might not remember me waking up, which would be better. I hurried through my shower so that she didn't start pounding on the door. For a girl, Margrite's quick. She took only ten minutes longer than I did, and by ten-thirty, we were out the door in search of breakfast. And our stuff.

"Where did you stash it?" she asked.

"The bus station."

"That was a good call," Margrite said.

"Why do you sound so surprised?" I didn't like the tone in her voice. "You're not the only one who can handle logistics."

"That's a nice fact to know, Aodan. I'll remember that next time I'm drowning in them."

We glared at each other and then laughed at the same time.

"I'm glad you're back."

She inhaled. "Me, too. That Eilor—"

I held up a hand. "Let's eat, and get the stuff, and then go somewhere we can't be overheard. Like somewhere with the door locked."

"Nervous?" A single brow went up.

"Yeah."

I glanced at her. She was studying me.

"Okay," she said.

We sat in silence as we grabbed coffee and a muffin in a small café. Then we headed to the station and retrieved the bags.

"Same place?" Margrite spoke finally.

I shook my head. "No. Let's go grab the bike while we're here and get out toward the edges of the city."

"All right."

And that was it. She knew when to ask for lots of details, and when to keep quiet. There would be time to talk later. Now it was about the logistics. So that we'd be ready for what was next.

Which made no sense. She was here, and she was safe. I was safe.

I just couldn't shake the unsettling feeling that this was an intermission, the calm before the storm that blew you to bits.

3

*N*ow that we had all the precious stuff, we needed my bike. I'd stashed it behind the last motel I'd stayed at with Margrite, right before Fangorn and I bolted to the Dragon Realm.

Yeah, listen to me, tossing that off like it's no big deal. I rolled my eyes at myself.

"We're going to need to cab it," I said.

"You couldn't have left it near here? Where is it?"

"The last place we stayed. Where Eilor found us," I added. I'd been talking to Fangorn, and Margrite had gone out to get a drink, or something. Eilor had kidnapped her there.

Margrite shuddered.

I looked at her. "I think you're going to need to tell me everything, too," I said.

She wouldn't look at me, and then she sighed. "Yeah, I guess so. I'd rather forget it, and him."

"I don't think that's possible."

"Are you going back there?"

"I could. I probably won't."

"Good," she said.

Good? How was that good? Shit. She hated the Dragon Realm. That 'good' was both intense and heartfelt. I couldn't go back without Margrite, but the place would kill her. Add on to that that she hated it—nope. That was it. No more Dragon Realm for me. I wasn't leaving my human family member here alone, with no one.

Since we were still near the bus station, there were cabs. We grabbed one, giving the driver the address to the motel. Then we sat.

I have never sat in uncomfortable silence with Margrite. We're best friends. We—well, I—tell her everything. She tells me nearly everything, or so she says. But this cab ride was super awkward.

She hated the Dragon Realm. That meant even if she could survive there, she didn't want to be there.

How would I ever be able to go back and even visit? They were family. And the way I felt when I was with them had no words. I'd been thinking about how to describe it to Margrite. Now it looked like I wouldn't be saying anything.

The heavy air in the cab increased. Finally, we made it to the motel, and I practically fell over my feet getting out of the car.

Jeesh. That sucked. This whole thing sucked. Just when I thought things might be improving, life gave me a big ol' nope. With a side of nope sauce.

Well, damn.

"You managed to keep the keys?"

She sounded amused. Was I the only one who was dying of discomfort?

"Of course. Come on, let's get out of here." I pulled the bike from where I'd hidden it among trash and bushes.

It's amazing. You can hide things in plain sight. Although I didn't expect this to still be here because it can be rolled away. I wasn't looking the gift horse in the mouth though.

I started it, and Margrite sat behind me, twisting as she hooked the two bags across each shoulder.

"I'm good," I heard in my ear.

Pulling out from the back lot, I felt eyes on me. The hair on my neck rose. Who was watching?

Well, let them try to catch me.

I drove out further from the downtown area, watching traffic and the buildings and businesses look better, more prosperous as we went out. I couldn't cross the city lines. I'd done it with Fangorn, and while he'd said there was no problem as I was with him, that didn't answer whether the curse or whatever was broken. My parents had a location spell on me—I called it the curse—and I could only leave the city with a family member. I'd discovered that when I was on this bike, trying to leave the city. That had been unpleasant, to say the least.

When I woke up this morning, I didn't think my outlook could get worse. Today was already testing that theory, and it wasn't even noon.

"There," Margrite pointed at a nice-looking motel with a couple of late-model cars. The rooms were small cottages.

I let her off at the office and took a drive around the property. This seemed nice. As I came around the front, she walked out.

"We are number four," waving toward the opposite corner. "I like it."

"Okay, let's get settled." I needed some kind of settling. I thought when I managed to hook back up with Margrite, a lot of my concerns would be solved.

Not so.

They were still there, and even more of a pain in my ass than before.

"I'm going to shower, like not-in-a-hurry-shower, and then I want to talk. I'm still hungry. Will you order something?" Margrite threw the last part over her shoulder.

Thankfully, the hotel provided a list of places where we

could get food delivered. Although I had to admit I was getting tired of eating out. Even in our ratty apartment, we were able to fix meals, and it was nice to not eat diner food, or fast food all the time.

Plus, it all smelled weird. Worse than I'd ever noticed before. Dragon nose at work. Kind of put your appetite off. However, Chinese sounded great, so I called and got the order working.

Margrite came out of the bathroom drying her hair. "Okay, who goes first?"

"What happened with Eilor?"

She sighed. "He grabbed me when I was going to get a soda. It was weird, A. I didn't notice him sneaking up behind me or anything. Just a flash of light, and then I felt something against my head. When I came to, I was in that stone house you found me in." She shrugged. "He fed me, although it was nasty. Bread and soup that made me want to gag. But he didn't give me a choice. I was tired, and weak all the time. I wanted to sleep. I think that's what I did, for the most part. I did try to stay awake though because he talked."

"He talked? What? To you?"

"No. He's one of those guys who likes to go through things. You know, like he should be journaling, or something? He really enjoys his own voice," her eyes rolled. "I think it's more than that, though. It's how he works through things, through planning."

"Well, it's interesting, but I'm not sure how that helps us right now."

"Is he dead?"

I looked over at her. Her face was uncharacteristically serious. "I don't think so."

"Damn it," her head dropped.

"M, what did he do to you?"

Margrite's eyes met mine. "He didn't touch me, didn't hurt me physically. I mean, outside the ropes he tied me with. They felt like steel! I tried to get out of them, and all it did was eat up my wrists," she held up her hands, showing the shadow of restraint marks. "But he told me about the place——"

"The Dragon Realm?" I had to work to keep my voice calm because the sight of her wrists made me furious. I could feel my dragon self wanting to burst out, burn him down. *Calm down*, I thought. *Eilor's not here.*

"The Fae Realm, and how someone like me wasn't welcome, and that you were so much more than a mere human like me could imagine. He asked me why, if we were family, I wanted to hold you back, keep you from your destiny. About how I was nothing, especially compared to you."

"Are you kidding me? He said that?"

She nodded. "Yes. And after a while, it started to make sense." Her last words were almost a whisper.

"That's crap, and you know it. You're my family."

"You have a lot of other family now."

"So?"

"I don't want to keep you from them."

"You're not. This is my home, this is my——"

"This?" Margrite gestured around her. "This, another one in a string of crappy no-tell motels? I saw that place. It was nice. They live differently there. You'd have a good life."

I shook my head. "You and I are family. We don't abandon family."

"But——"

"No. Not even a conversation."

"You didn't enjoy being there? Being a dragon?"

I opened my mouth to reply and stopped. Yes, I'd enjoyed being a dragon. It was like nothing else I'd ever experienced. I didn't have the words to explain how much I'd enjoyed it.

It was like my soul was where it was supposed to be.

"Yes, I enjoyed it. I mean, I'm still klutzy, but I liked it. I liked the other dragons."

"What about the people? Eilor told me there were people—fae——"

"I liked them, too. Although I was more comfortable with the dragons," I added. "I met my sister."

"What was she like?" Margrite's earlier concern was forgotten. "Oh my God, tell me about her."

"She's really pretty, and she has dark hair like me. She's married to, are you ready for this? The Dragon King."

"A dragon is king?"

"No, he's the king of the Dragon Realm. He's funny—he used to be human—and I think they're happy. Aine? She's..." I thought about my sister. She didn't seem real. "She's serious and doesn't take anything from anyone. She's sarcastic, and she and Fangorn are really close."

Margrite studied me for a minute. "You okay?"

I shrugged. "I am. It's weird, coming into this family who is all rah, rah family when it's been you and me for years. Before that, it was only Tina and us," I felt the ache in my heart I always did at the thought of my foster mom.

Margrite patted my shoulder. "We always bitched about no family, or no family that gave a shit about us. But a family that cares about each other has problems, too, A. All family does."

"You and I are family. Everyone else has to earn a place."

"Even Fangorn?"

"Even Fangorn. He helped me get you back, but I think part of it was because he knew that I'd have to go back to the Dragon Realm with him, and that was his goal."

"Well, I'm glad you had agendas that matched up." She grinned a lopsided grin. "You did order food, didn't you? Let's save anything else for after I've eaten and finished getting ready. I swear, all I want to do is eat."

What else had being in the Realms done to her? "Okay," I said.

She went into the bathroom and closed the door firmly behind her. I lay back on the bed, closing my eyes.

I must have fallen asleep. Because I sure wasn't in the Cavern of the Ancients. And not with it full of dragons.

The air was tense. There was roaring, but it seemed like all the dragons were arguing in the collective. I couldn't hear it, or what was being said. I was watching all the dragons, marveling at the many colors, and varying sizes. There were a lot more dragons than the ones I'd seen. Fangorn said there were only eleven, including him. These didn't look like the dragons I'd met.

I jumped when one, a tall green dragon, stood up on his—I thought it was male—hind legs and opened his mouth and roared, a plume of flame rising along the walls of the cavern.

All the other dragons stopped, watching.

The very air waited.

"We must make the change," he said.

There was an answering roar--of outrage, or agreement, I couldn't tell. My eyes flew open.

Someone was knocking on the door, pounding on it.

Oh, right. The food. I let myself relax as I rolled off the bed. I peeked out of the peephole, and as I thought, there was a delivery guy. I knew that I was being paranoid, but I didn't trust anyone here.

I shoved cash into the guy's hand, and took the bag, closing the door behind me and locking it again. I wasn't going to be easy until we got away from here.

Caleb and Stefan were still a problem. I didn't know, still, who had set up our building, or who had been looking for me when Margrite was hiding at the diner. There was someone here who was a threat. The place we'd called home for five years had been destroyed by thugs—and for the first time, I couldn't tell whose thugs they were. That was a problem.

Until we got out of this city, we were in danger. That wasn't a big deal—I was in danger a lot of the time. It's part of being a thief and stealing for a living. But I didn't know who it was threatening me and Margrite, and that was a problem.

You can't outwit or defeat the enemy you can't see.

I could go back to the Dragon Realm but that would leave

Margrite exposed and alone, and that was something I wasn't going to do.

Even with all my mental gymnastics, we were back to the place where we'd been before I woke up as a dragon. We had to get out of here, and we had to do it before someone got hold of us and hurt or killed us.

Which brought me back to the problem I'd had before I met Fangorn. The spell. It had stopped me from leaving the city limits more than once. Now that I'd met Eilor, and had some idea of what my parents were worried about, I got it. It made my life a lot harder, though.

Damn it all to hell and back. I was going to have to call him, ask him to escort me out of here. And somehow, I was going to need to get away from his agenda, no matter how much it made sense to me, or how much I wanted to be part of whatever—anything—the dragons were doing.

I couldn't tell Margrite, but I'd never felt better, or more *right*, than when I was with them, even with my obvious lack of being one with my dragon fu, as Margrite referred to it.

In the last week, I've learned that everything I have ever known was… well, not an entire lie, but a lot of exaggerations. First, and what seemed most important to me, my mom wasn't a druggie, or a junkie, or whatever she'd been characterized as. She'd given me up because she was dying. At least, that was what Fangorn, my grandfather said.

Fangorn is an interesting name because Fangorn is an interesting guy. He looks like a man, but he's a dragon. He can shift into fae, which is an entirely different race from us humans. He lives in the Dragon Realm, which is part of the Fae Realm, or what he calls the Realms. It's a parallel world to this one.

And that means that I'm part fae, and part dragon, in addition to being part human. My mom was human. My dad was half fae, half dragon, and he could shift like Fangorn does. Except my dad lived as a fae, and he escaped to this world, our world. The Human Realm. There's a guy in the Realms—his name is Eilor—and he wants dragon-fae shifters. He has some grand plan for an army and total domination. Or something like that. I wasn't exactly sure what his plan was.

You would think in a parallel world where they have magic, fae, shifters, trolls, goblins—the bad guys could get a little more creative. But nope. Eilor wants world domination and any and all the power possible.

He has a brother in this Realm—Stefan—who was the crime lord boss of my worst enemy, Caleb. He wanted me, or the crazy box I'd stolen that set this whole thing in motion. The box, I'd learned, was a portal, and it allowed people to travel between the Realms. Stefan had showed up when Eilor had come to meet me, demanding the box. So. We had Eilor, with who knew how many crazy plans. His scary ass brother, Stefan, who wanted the magic box ride back to the Realms. Caleb, who would like to kill me just because. The Realms, which I loved, but would kill my best friend. My entire new family that was a major jumble of fae, human, and dragon. None of whom lived in the same place I did. Oh, and the location curse thingy—whatever it was. The thing that wouldn't let me leave the boundaries of this city.

I'd wanted to do this on my own, figure out what to do for Margrite and I, and get us away and somewhere safe. But there were so many people who were doing their damnedest to screw that up for us.

Damn it. Our choices were narrowing fast.

4

*M*argrite came out of the bathroom, tucking things into a small bag. "Oh, good. Food's here. How is it I'm starving again?"

I pushed the carton over toward the other chair at the small table. "Bon appetit."

She laughed and sat with me. "You okay?"

"Why?" It came out muffled, because my mouth was full of lo mein.

"I don't know, you look weird."

I shrugged and kept eating. I wasn't going to get into it. My head was already full of snarls and tangles.

Margrite turned on the TV, switching to the news. She loved the news—local, cable, all of it. When I made fun of her, she called me a philistine, and ignored my teasing. She sat down and pulled out her phone. Her breath caught. "Oh, no."

"What?" I could feel all my senses go on alert at the tone in her voice.

"We need to go and see Nala," she said.

"What?" I forced myself to inhale deeply, so that my racing heart would slow.

"I normally go in and help her a couple of mornings, remember? I haven't been there in—what day is it?"

"Wednesday."

"In over a week." Margrite glared at me. "That was her, leaving like ten texts, wondering if I was all right."

"What? This isn't my fault."

"You and your dragon," she muttered in the direction of her phone.

I rolled my eyes and went on eating. What, like I couldn't hear her? She had some kind of invisible wall of privacy around her? I also couldn't help my dragon. Besides, I liked him.

"Nala? It's Margrite."

Whatever Nala was saying, I could hear it from here. Not the words, but the tone, and how loud she was speaking.

"Hey, hey—slow down. Tell me again," Margrite commanded.

At that, I looked over. Margrite was nodding, her brows furrowed. She saw me watching her and glared at me again.

Whatever was going on, somehow this was going to be my fault. I could just tell. May as well eat while I could.

"Why did she say that? Why would she come to you?" Margrite asked.

Silence as she listened to Nala, and then she said, "Okay. We'll come by tomorrow, and we'll meet her there. Nowhere else, and you have to be there, too."

Nala said something and Margrite cut her off. "There is no one else we can trust, Nala. If it doesn't happen like this, then it doesn't happen."

Then she said, "Yeah, this is a good number for me right now. If something changes, let me know. If not, don't call. We'll be there tomorrow."

She hung up.

"What?" I asked.

"I don't even know where to start," Margrite said slowly. "You know your—our—case worker?"

"Marion?" I said. I was shocked. I hadn't seen her since I'd been emancipated. That wasn't true—I'd gone back to see her about six months after that, so she could know that I was still alive, still okay. She'd cried at my hearing and she'd been my only caseworker. As I got older, I realized how rare that was. Most kids in the system had at least one change. But I hadn't. Marion had been there since my mom got sick. She'd met my mom, although when I asked her about it, she had said she didn't know her well. The last time I'd asked, her eyes filled with tears, so I didn't ask again.

I figured she had information I didn't really want to know about my mom. No one wants to hear how their parent died.

"What about her?"

"She came to Nala, looking for you and me."

"What? How the hell does she know Nala?"

"That was my question."

"And why is she looking for me now?"

"My next question," Margrite said.

"All this—whatever it is," I waved my hands, "Keeps getting weirder and weirder. What did you agree to do?"

She sighed. "I said that we'd come by Nala's shop and meet with Marion. Right after it opens, at ten. Nala said it won't be super busy and we can talk."

"What is there to talk about?" I couldn't figure it out. "Why now, after five years? It's not like we left, or have been totally out of sight." She could have found us. She'd been around long enough that she knew the streets her kids lived in.

"Right? It doesn't make sense."

"If I'm being fair, nothing the past week or so has made sense. I mean, I can breathe fire," I added with a smile.

"Can you fly?" Margrite changed the subject.

"Yes."

"How is it?"

"Like the most amazing thing ever," I said before I could help myself.

The most extraordinary expression came over Margrite's face. Longing, envy, sadness and happiness. It happened so fast that I wasn't sure I'd seen what I thought I had. Particularly given her initial reaction to the Realms.

"That sounds wonderful."

"It was. I'll have to take you with me," I said.

She smiled. It was the first genuine smile I'd seen since I'd met her in front of the book shop. "I'd like that."

"Okay, that's under future business. We need to figure out what we're going to do."

"Let's finish this—" she gestured at the food, "And then we'll talk about it. I want to get this out of the room."

"What, you don't love the smell of leftover Chinese?"

"Shut up," she said.

We finished our lunch and then I bagged up all the empties and headed outside for the dumpster. I took the opportunity to walk around the motel, seeing what I could see.

There was a car on the corner opposite the motel that looked like it had a couple of people in it. They could be just hanging out, or doing a drug deal, or some other business that had nothing to do with me, right?

Nevertheless, I hurried back to the room.

"Okay, what do you want to do?" Margrite asked as I came in.

"I want to get the hell out of here."

"Still?"

"Why not? Let's meet with Marion tomorrow, and we can book flights right after we talk to her."

"Why not now?"

"Because we don't have a good track record with keeping our flights," I said with a laugh. "So, let's see what drama she's got for us, and then leave."

Slowly, Margrite nodded. "Let's figure out what flights we can get in the next day or so. You know, if you can get out of here."

I sighed. "I'll call him, after we talk to Marion, and tell him he needs to escort me, if that's what needs to happen."

"You think he'll just do it? Just like that?"

"He's not the enemy, M. We're just … we just have different agendas."

She looked at me, and then said, "Your family. You get to manage them."

We spent the rest of the evening looking up the flights that would get us to the islands, and how to manage the various legs.

All we needed to do was get through whatever Marion wanted, and then we were out of here. I know that I had more things to consider, but since Margrite couldn't come with me, there was nothing else to consider. We were going to go through with our original plan.

Nothing else would get in our way. I'd contact Fangorn, have him escort me out of the city, and we'd be gone.

I hoped.

5

$\mathcal{W}$hen I woke the next morning, I felt good for the first time in a long time. I ignored the fact that being with my dragon family made me feel amazing. I'd noticed that I could feel them, in the back of my mind, all the time. It made me feel part of something. I shook my head. That wasn't part of my future. At least, not right now. I hadn't dreamed the dream of the crystal, or falling to my death, so that was good, too. I'd kept the door in my mind closed, even though I could sense the other dragons behind it.

Margrite and I had a plan. Once we met with Nala and Marion, I'd talk with Fangorn, and have him get me outside of the city limits. Then we'd book our flights, and we'd be out of here.

Finally, we'd be able to live the life we wanted, and without all the crap we'd been putting up with the past five years.

It was only five years, but it seemed a lifetime. I'd been a foster kid from the age of two until eighteen. I'd met Margrite in middle school when we'd both been trying to steal the same wallet. She and I were best friends from almost that moment on. She was in the foster system too, so when she realized that my foster mom, Tina, was normal, and didn't hit, drink (she used to, but she stopped), or any of the shit that foster parents are always accused of, she hung out with us a lot.

And for a couple of years, things were great. Until Tina was killed when I was in tenth grade. I moved in with Margrite's foster family and the second I turned eighteen, I went to court and claimed the money that Tina had left me.

I thanked my lucky stars that Tina had been the one I ended up with. She wasn't perfect, but she tried, all the time. She got sober, and by the time she died, I called her Mom. Because she was the only mom I'd ever known. She left me everything. Not that I could touch it—no way. The state wouldn't let that happen. I had to be eighteen. But Marion, my case worker, oversaw it for me with a competence and dedication I later learned wasn't always duplicated in her fellow workers. She was amazing.

That little stash of money formed the basis for what Margrite and I were trying to do now. We'd planned then, after I aged out. We'd save money, and then we'd get the hell out of here. Five years later, we had the money. We'd picked out a house. We had all the paperwork we needed. All that was left to do was to get out.

That whole location spell thing was a pain in my ass.

I knew that my parents were worried about someone trying to steal me, but this made my life a ton harder now that I was grown. They didn't feel they had a choice though. Lionel, my dad, knew that Eilor—the same jerk who'd taken Margrite, who'd try to capture me and use me for who knew what—was after them. He was obsessed with the children of dragon shifters.

And there weren't many. There were eleven dragons left. My dad had made it twelve, but Eilor killed him. Aine and I had brought the numbers up to thirteen. Of the thirteen of us, only Fangorn and I could shift. And we had some badass magic. Well, the other dragons did. I hoped I'd eventually learn it and be able to use it without killing myself. The magic tended to show up when it wanted to, and I had no input on what happened.

So of course, Eilor wanted to use that. The dragon magic. I was the weakest link, in his mind.

I sighed. If this was anyone but Marion, I'd say to hell with it and ignore her. But Marion had been one of the few adults who had always been good to me. She'd proved over and over that she worried about me, and what was best for me.

And Margrite adored Nala. We were stuck going through with this. To me, it felt like one more roadblock that had yet unknown consequences. Plus, Nala would probably ask me about the tarot reading she'd done for me, and I didn't need any more woo woo in my life than there was already.

I wondered how Marion had found Nala. One more thing to ask.

Margrite burst back in, a couple of bags in her hand. "How about a breakfast taco?"

"That sounds amazing. Tell me you have coffee, too."

"Of course."

She handed me a bag and a large to go coffee. "What do you think Nala and Marion want?"

I shrugged. "Dunno. What I want to know is how they met. Did we introduce them at some point?"

"No. Nala told me that Marion came into her shop, looking for us."

"That's weird," I frowned into my taco.

"We'll know soon enough."

"And then the islands," I said.

We grinned at each other. It was finally here. Finally.

After breakfast, we headed out to Nala's shop. We got there right after it opened as Marion had requested.

The little bell tinkled as the door opened.

"Nala?" Margrite asked.

Nala flew out of the back room and enveloped Margrite in a

hug. "Where have you been? You missed two days, and I had no idea where you were!"

I could tell that Nala's emotion took Margrite by surprise.

"Um," Margrite glanced at me.

I understood. How do you tell someone what had happened to us?

"I had to take care of some stuff," Margrite said. "I'm so sorry. I didn't think you'd worry."

"I always worry about the people I care about," Nala stepped back, her hands still on Margrite's shoulders. "Now come on back. Marion's here. I gotta tell you, girl, my worry, which was already high, went into high gear when that lady showed up."

She walked to the back room, pushing aside the curtain and then holding it so we could follow her. It was the same room that we'd been in for the reading.

I wondered if Margrite would tell her that the reading had come true. That it was right in some respects. I thought Nala might not gloat like M would.

But maybe there were a lot of other things for Margrite to worry about.

"Aodan! Margrite! It's so good to see you both!" Marion got up from the chair she'd been sitting in, arms outstretched.

We both hugged her.

"You both look good," Marion said. "A little tired, but good."

"That's accurate," I said. "Marion, what's going on? Why did you come looking for us?"

She sighed, and instantly, ten years landed right on her face. "Because it was time for me to find you and tell you the truth."

I blinked. What?

Margrite was faster, thank God. "What truth?"

Marion gave her a half-smile. "The whole truth."

"Why don't you all sit down?" Nala came around behind

me. "Things are easier when everyone isn't standing around awkwardly. And then I'll leave you be," she added.

Marion held up a hand. "No, you should be here. I know from talking with you that this won't seem so far out there to you, and you care about Margrite like I do. If it's all right with the two of you," she looked from Margrite to me, "I'd like Nala to stay."

"I don't have any idea what you're talking about," I said. "But I don't care if Nala is here."

Margrite nodded.

We all sat and then looked at Marion. After all, this was her show.

"I have to go back, Aodan, to when you first came into the foster system."

Great. It's old home week, and we're going to drag up the druggie mom. Even though I knew she wasn't a drug addict, I didn't want to hear it again. Somehow, knowing the truth from Fangorn was worse. I was thinking about how to tell Marion— nicely—that I wasn't interested when she continued.

"Everything I told you was a lie."

That stopped all my thoughts. "What?" It annoyed me that word was on my most-used list today.

"I knew your mom. I knew her well—really well. She was my best friend," tears filled Marion's eyes. "I did what she wanted, but I didn't want to."

"Start at the beginning." I nearly didn't recognize my own voice. It was hard and on the verge of anger.

Out of the corner of my eye, I saw Nala take Margrite's hand. I didn't take my eyes off Marion.

Marion sighed. She wasn't bothered by my anger. She'd seen it a lot. "We grew up together—we were the two M's in our neighborhood—and she told me when she met Lionel. I met him, later, after they'd been dating for a while. He was..." her eyes clouded.

I could tell she wasn't seeing any of us.

"He was the most amazing man I'd ever met, and I loved that he loved your mother. It was like a light lit up in both when they were together. They were devoted to one another," she looked back at me, smiling. A tear tracked down her cheek.

"They got married quickly, and then in what seemed only a few minutes, she was calling me to tell me she was pregnant." Marion sighed again. "I was so happy for them, but so worried. Maria told me that Lionel's family didn't approve, although I didn't realize then how much of an understatement that was."

She looked at the three of us. "How much do you know about your family, Aodan? I mean, the truth?"

"All of it," I said.

Marion gave a little nod.

"I have no idea what you're talking about," Nala said.

"I'll tell you later," Margrite said, "If that's okay."

I nodded. "What do you know about my family?" I asked Marion.

"A lot of it. Maria didn't tell me until, well, until right before they disappeared. She told me that Lionel was really worried about someone that was looking for him. Edward, something that starts with an E?" Her eyebrows went up.

"Eilor," I said.

"Yes, that's it. Eilor. And then, at the end of the pregnancy, she and Lionel both vanished. I filed a missing person report and I was so worried, because she had shared some of what Ei—Eilor was after," she stumbled over the unfamiliar name.

"He's still around, and he's still an asshole," I said.

"Oh my God," Marion breathed. "You have to get away. That guy is—"

"Toxic," said Margrite.

"Yes. Maria got in touch with me when she came back, and she only had you with her, Aodan. She was so sad, and she had a tough time dealing with reality. I helped her a lot because she really struggled. She loved you so much, and she missed your sister terribly." Her eyes filled with tears again.

"What happened to her?"

"After she'd been back about a year, it was obvious that she was getting sick, that something inside was just taking the life from her. She thought it was because of the time she spent … over there." Marion waved a hand, glancing at Nala as she did so. "But she got weaker and weaker, and I ended up renting two apartments next to each other for us, so I could be there when she needed help."

"Why did you let me go into the system?" I asked. My voice was hard. All I could see was all the shit I'd suffered as a foster kid, all the things that had happened, all the people who had hurt me.

"I was working for them by then. Maria told me that Eilor was obsessed, and he'd never stop. He took Aine from her. He had plans that were…"

"Disgusting," I finished it for her.

She nodded. "Very much. And she was so afraid for you. She was afraid that whatever happened to her there, it had come here, and that somehow, Eilor would find her again. She knew she was dying, that she had to do something to protect you when she wasn't there to do it." Her voice broke, and she dropped her head. Her shoulders shook a little.

I realized she was crying. Some of my anger ebbed away. Whatever else, this was someone that knew and loved my mom. Both my parents. That wasn't fake.

Marion looked up. "She gave you up. She felt that if we put you into the foster system, under the name that Lionel used here, that it would be harder for you to find. And she was right. No one found you, until recently, did they?"

"How do you know that?" I asked. My guard and my suspicions were on high alert again.

Marion leaned over and picked up her purse. She dug into it and came out with a small box, the kind that jewelry comes in.

The room was so quiet that a hair could have dropped on the floor and we all would have heard it. Nala and Margrite had been quiet while Marion talked, and I could tell that Margrite was dying to ask questions. So was I, but I wanted to see what was in the box.

Marion opened it and took out a ring. It was a small gold ring, but it looked more like a man's ring than a woman's. Just because the band was thicker than you saw with women's rings. It had a clear stone in the middle, a stone that I bet was a diamond. It was probably two, two and half carats, I thought, looking at it with my thief eye.

"Lionel made this for Maria. She said that when she wore it, she could talk to him somehow."

My gaze flew to Margrite. I hadn't gotten around to asking her if she had the necklace, mostly because if she did, I didn't want to know. I didn't want to have to lie to Fangorn.

Marion continued, "She said that now that she was back, and away from him, and all the other parts of that life, she didn't wear it, or notice anything. But she said that Lionel had planned to make one for you and Aine so that the four of you would always be able to be in contact. She also said that she thought it was tied to you, somehow," she held the ring out to me.

"She said when she wore it after you were born, she would see things sometimes that looked like what a baby might see. So, she took it off—"

"Why?" Margrite asked.

"I think it was painful. A reminder of all that she'd lost, and all that she could still lose," Marion said. She gazed at Margrite, no apology in her words.

Even though I didn't like that my mom had somehow given up, I liked that Marion was her friend even now. Taking no shit from anyone about her friend. That was what a true friend did.

"She told me to keep it, and to check on it. That if something was going on with you, she thought it might change. She didn't tell me how, and honestly, this was right before—well, right before she passed away. Honestly, I didn't know how true this was, or how much of it really made sense. She wasn't in a place that invited a lot of in-depth discussion."

"How did she die?"

"She just sort of … she went to sleep, and she didn't wake up. The police … well, I had to call them. I told them I'd gone to do a well check on her, since she'd given you up and I was worried—they thought it was drugs."

"Why didn't you tell them that wasn't true?"

Marion shrugged.

I wanted to punch her. All my calm had left and gone somewhere else.

"She knew she was dying, Aodan. Her worry, and my worry, was for you. She gave you to me so that you'd be safe. So that I'd be your case worker. Maria wasn't stupid! She knew what happened to kids in the system—"

"Kind of like what happened to me?" I got up and walked away from the table. My heart pounded in my ears, and I could feel my stomach rolling around like it did right before you threw up.

"I'm sorry. I did the best I could. I couldn't let them know I knew her, or you. They would have removed me as your case worker. Then I couldn't do anything for you."

"You let her just die?" I whirled around, wanting to hurt someone, to get some answers.

"She was always going to die," Marion said.

"What does this have to do with right now?" Margrite interrupted. "You told Nala you needed to talk to Aodan—to us. Why?"

"I wanted to tell you the truth. I keep tabs on you, mostly through you," Marion nodded at Margrite. "I noticed that you weren't in here for over a week, and I got concerned. Plus, in the last week, the ring, well" she looked down at the box in front of me. "I've kept it on a chain and worn it since you aged out. Maria insisted I not tell you unless I needed to, and I struggled with that." She looked down, and when she looked up, there were tears on her face. "The last five years, I've wanted to tell you, and it was too hard to think I was breaking almost the last promise I made my best friend. Anyway," she held up a hand as I started to speak, "The ring has been … well, it's been like it's woken up. I knew that something had happened. I came to see Nala, and she told me she was worried as well. I was so relieved that she called me last night and told me you'd called."

"Say what you need to say," I said. My heart still beat fast and sweat was beading along my neck at my collar.

"I need you to know that your mom loved you, and she stayed here as long as she could, trying to set things up for you."

"How can I leave the city?" I asked. If Marion knew about my dad, and the truth of where he was from, of who he was, maybe she knew how to break the spell.

"That is still in effect?" Shock showed on her face.

"In a big way," I said. "Like knock me on my ass."

"He's serious," Margrite added.

I glared at her, coming to sit back down. We didn't need to go into that now.

"Um, I … I don't know. I'm not sure. Maria might have left it in the box she left with me—"

"You have my mom's things?" The rage that had just started to settle in me flared up again. "I want it."

Marion's eyes narrowed, and her brows came together, a sure sign that she was losing her temper. It didn't happen often, but when she did, she took no shit from whoever pissed her off.

I hated seeing that expression come over her face normally, but now I didn't care.

"She—"

"Was my mom. And you had a lifetime with her. I had two years, and then she gave me away. I want to see what she left." My tone did not invite discussion.

Marion met my gaze, and then sighed, looking away. "All right. Take the ring. I'll get it and bring it back here."

"Today," I said.

"I do have a job, Aodan."

"And you're out doing welfare checks," I shot back. "Get it. We'll wait."

"Take the ring," she pushed the box with it toward me. "That is definitely yours."

Without taking my eyes off her I closed the box and slid it into my pocket. I'd look at it later, when I wasn't in front of an audience. If something was going to happen when I touched it, I didn't want to know right now.

Marion got up, brushing at her eyes, and left, shoving the curtain aside roughly. A moment later, I heard the bell on the front door jangle.

6

"*Y*ou were hard on her," Nala said.

"You don't know anything about it," I said.

"I know more than you think. She was frantic when she came in last night. She hides it well, but I could feel her anxiety about you."

"Yeah, she's been so anxious she never told me anything about this."

"Because it killed your mom," Margrite said.

I looked at her. "What do you mean?"

"Your mom loved your dad so much that she let it kill her. She lost one of her kids, and she came back here, and she was dying from whatever he, or that place," Margrite spat out the words, "Did to her. Marion was her best friend, and she saw that. You think she wanted that for you? She loves you, A."

"Yeah, whatever," I didn't want to hear it.

"You're so stupid sometimes. I've always seen it, and I thought it was weird, because my other case workers never gave a shit about me like she did with you. Ever. I was jealous that she cared so much. I was so glad she got me assigned to her cases after Tina died."

Jeesh. We were hitting all the buttons today, weren't we?

"I don't pretend to know what you're talking about, but I want to ask if things you saw while you were wherever—" Nala made a motion with one of her hands, "Fell in line with the tarot reading?"

"I don't know," Margrite said. "We spent most of the week in two different places."

"Why?" I asked. This seemed a little off based on what just happened.

"Because the deck you pulled?" Nala looked between us.

I gave her a short nod.

"It's been popping up when I reach for a deck out of my basket," Nala leaned over and brought out a large rather ratty looking woven basket with decks of cards held together with ribbon. "I was thinking of you two, wondering how you were, because I hadn't seen you," She smiled briefly at Margrite. "And the deck exploded out of my hands. I got concerned, what with not seeing you, and then Marion came to see me yesterday."

"It's been a difficult week," Margrite said.

She was choosing her words carefully. I appreciated it.

"Can you tell me? Can I help?" Nala asked.

Her manner, her tone, everything about her was calm. She looked serene, and I envied it. I couldn't get a hold of my emotions, because with everything that Marion told us, I'd been up and then down and then way down.

And while she told me about my mom, she didn't really give me an idea of how to get the hell out of here.

"I want to, but I think if we do, it may put you in danger," Margrite answered for the both of us.

Nala gave her a searching look.

"I'm serious."

Nala didn't answer. Then she said, "Let me get you something to drink while we wait. I need a drink, but it's too early in the morning to break out the whiskey," she went into a room that was beyond the one where we sat, shaking her head.

"Was that all right?" Margrite leaned into me.

"Yeah, I don't think we need to tell her."

"What about Marion?"

I took a deep breath. I didn't know what to think. "I think I'll get some more information about my mom. Do you think she told Marion the whole truth?"

"It sounds like it. It makes sense to me."

I pulled the box with the ring in it out of my pocket. "What the hell is this?"

Margrite shook her head. "I don't know. I don't understand all the things that go on in that place. It scares me. All these things, the past week—" she waved her hands, "These are supposed to be the things we read about in a fairy tale or whatever. But, like a Grimm fairy tale where everyone might die. I'd never thought I'd experience a fairy tale in real life."

I took the ring out of the box and dumped it into my hand. It felt warm, alive.

Like the necklace.

The necklace!

I leaned close to Margrite. "Did you take what I thought you took when Eilor sent you back?"

Her eyes got wide. "You saw that?"

"Come on, M. This is me. I know you, I know your tells."

Her lips pursed. "I did."

"Where is it?"

"Hidden."

"In your stuff?"

"Does it matter?"

"Are you kidding? Did you hear Fangorn before Eilor took you? He wants that thing back!"

"You're going to tell him?"

"Don't be stupid," I said. "I saw it, and I didn't say a word. I wasn't sure, so I asked. But I didn't say anything to anyone. I can't believe that you would think I would."

She didn't answer right away. "Well," she looked down. "Things are different."

"How are they different?" I felt my neck get hot. "It's still you and me—"

"And all the family you have over—over there!" She threw her hand out. "I know what's over there!"

"No, you really don't," I said. "But it doesn't matter. Where am I? What am I planning to do?"

"You have so much that is over there for you," Margrite sounded frustrated.

"And my family is here," I said hoping she could hear the sincerity in my words. "Margrite, you're right. I didn't have to come back. I chose to. You and I are all we have. Sure, I have other family—" I felt a pang at my dragon being unable to be with the others again, but I pushed it down. "But that doesn't mean I drop the only family I've ever known. I don't want to."

My dragon woke and pushed back at my words. He didn't like it. He was a dragon, and he belonged with other dragons. Without having to be told, I knew that something of him—of me—would die without them.

She looked at me, not speaking. I could tell she was weighing what she heard. While Margrite might keep some things from me—another discussion that still bothered me—I didn't lie to her. I never had. Not since the first day we'd met when she caught me in the middle of pick-pocketing.

Then she sighed. "I don't want you to miss out on something you deserve."

"Why would you expect that I'd up and leave? We're leaving, but we're going to where we planned. Nothing has changed."

"Everything has changed, Aodan!"

I shook my head. "Not enough for us to make changes. Maybe Marion can actually help me break the spell." My dragon roared in my head, so loud that I was sure the others must have heard him. He didn't like what I was saying.

We stopped as Nala came back in with a tray, of all things. A teapot and cups were on it, and I could see steam rising from the pot.

I didn't even know the last time I had tea. *Relax*, I said to my dragon. *Relax. Not the place to burst out.*

While this was out of the ordinary for me, it didn't seem to be for anyone else. When Nala set the tray down, Margrite immediately poured tea while Nala added a dollop of honey to it.

"What is it?" Margrite asked.

"A chamomile mix. I think calming is a pleasant thing to aim for," Nala said with half a grin.

In that moment, I could see what Margrite saw in the fortune telling woo woo woman. For all the crystals and incense and those damn cards, she radiated good energy.

I'd always noticed if someone was good or bad based on the vibes I got from them. After I'd shifted for the first time, I could tell this sense was heightened. Being in the room with Eilor in the Dragon Realm nearly made me sick. He was definitely full of bad vibes.

"Calm would be nice," I said as I picked up my cup. It did smell good.

God almighty. They were going to convert me. Next thing you know, I'd be wearing a crystal and carrying weeds tied with a special string in my pocket. The dragon relaxed within me; I could feel the release of tension like the breaking of a rubber band.

The bell over the front door rang out sharply, like the person coming in opened the door hard. I could hear footsteps; then Marion appeared, pushing the curtain aside.

"Let me take that," Nala jumped up to grab a box Marion carried under her arm.

"No, this is for Aodan," Marion said. "Take it," She added to me.

I carefully cradled the box as she handed it toward me. It was heavy.

"What is it?"

Marion didn't ask, sitting down and accepting a cup from Nala. She took a sip and then said, "A bunch of stuff from your mom. Journals, pictures. Baby books for you and Aine. And directions."

"For?"

"How to break your location spell." Marion dropped that like she was handing me a tissue.

"What? You can do that?"

"I can. Your mom made me... well, the best word would be a guardian. When you were ready, when you wanted to leave for the right reasons, or because you needed to, I was to help you. She handed over the responsibility to me."

"Are you part of the Realms?" I asked.

Margrite started next to me but I ignored her. I knew I was taking a risk by talking in front of Nala, but what the hell? Nala already knew there was some wonky stuff at work. She didn't know the details, but I suppose with her line of work, she was prepared to take some information on faith. Or not—it didn't matter.

Marion shook her head. "As best as I can understand it, your father allowed Maria to share in some of his abilities, or whatever. She gave that to me. I can only do the things she allowed me to. And I'm happy to help you."

"Why didn't you tell me this before?"

"I told you, I thought you were happy. I didn't know you wanted to leave. I kept tabs on you the best I could—because your mom was clear that you might never have anything like your dad did. And if that was the case she wanted you to grow up normal."

"Now I'm abnormal?"

"Stop being difficult," Marion said, and I heard the woman I'd known for as long as I could remember in those three words.

I didn't know what was so tough about this. I was able to forgive Fangorn even though I was sure he wasn't telling me everything and had his own agenda. Why was I being so hard on Marion?

Because she knew me. Knew what I'd gone through, lived through. Knew better than to keep things to herself that might help me or give me a leg up.

However, she was here. And she wanted to help me.

"What do we need to do?"

"We need to release the holding spell," Marion said.

"What do you need for that?" Nala asked.

Marion smiled. "I have the things I need. It's not a lot, and not what we think of as magic here. It's just a stone."

I knew it. I knew crystals were going to come into this before it was all done.

Margrite must have known what I was thinking because she nudged me.

"Shut it," I whispered.

"May I see it?" Nala asked. "Once you find it? I do have an affinity with stone," she added with a smile.

Everyone looked at me.

"Is that allowed?" I asked Marion.

She shrugged. "Your mom only told me not to broadcast this, but not that it would burn limbs off anyone else who touched it."

"Well, that's a good thing. I need all mine," Nala said lightly.

I opened the box. "What does it look like?"

"It's blue with green." Marion replied.

I fished around, moving the books and envelopes. The stone was wedged in a corner, looking like nothing special at all.

Until I took it and wrapped my fingers around it.

7

---

*I*mmediately I lost sight of the small back room at the woo woo shop. I was in a stone room, a lot like the one where Eilor had been hiding out, where I'd gone to bargain with him for Margrite.

A tall, dark-haired man leaned over me. I realized with a shock that I was seeing someone else's memories as they did—not as an observer, but as though I were them.

Okay. Who was this guy, and who was I?

"Doll," he said. "You need to take this and listen carefully."

"I don't know that I can," she—I? —said.

Her voice was soft, and I could hear the thread of worry in it. I could feel that she was exhausted and tired from running and fighting and—birth.

Oh, God.

I needed to put the stone down, but that didn't seem possible. I couldn't move her—our—limbs.

The man—that meant this was my dad—took her hands. "You can. You have dragon blood because of the kids, and because of the ring, and because of that last bit."

What was the last bit? While I was pondering that, he continued talking.

"I am so tired, Line," she said.

He pulled her to him and wrapped his arms around her. I could feel them. They were strong and there was something else, something that hummed within him.

"But you need to listen, because this will be important to the kids, especially to Aodan," he leaned back and looked in her eyes, and I felt like he could see me. Like he knew I was here.

"Why only Aodan?"

"I don't know. I can't tell. But I know that he's going to need to know this."

"They're so little," she whispered.

As one, their heads turned, and they looked toward the opposite wall. There was a large cradle, and in it I could see two bundles of blankets wrapped in that baby burrito fashion. Both the burritos had dark hair sticking out, and it was hard for me to realize that I was seeing me, me and Aine.

Oh my God.

"They're going to be great, Mari," he said, walking away from her—me. He leaned over the crib and ran a hand over the heads of both the burritos. "They're so strong." Then he turned to look at her, crossing his arms.

"That's why we have to do this, and you have to be strong, too."

I could feel Mom—my heart broke a little even thinking that —start to cry. "I'm just so tired, and this place is so evil. It seeps into me and totally sucks the life out of me."

He walked toward her and enveloped her once again. "It's going to be okay, sweetie. I prom—"

"Aodan!"

I looked around, and I was in Nala's back room.

"What the hell happened?" I asked. I knew what happened, but I was worried about what had happened to me, sitting here.

Given what I knew about the dragons' collective consciousness, I knew why I was seeing this. It was weird that it happened when I held the stone, but this was the sharing. Fangorn hadn't mentioned that you could do it with objects. I knew the necklace that Margrite had was infused with Fangorn's blood. Did that mean the stone was as well?

With something that felt like horror, I looked at the blue-green stone. It didn't look like it had a blood middle or anything.

So how was it happening? *Fangorn*, I thought, letting the door open. *Did you see this?*

"You went away," Margrite answered me. "You were here, but you weren't. And you were talking although I couldn't hear everything you said. You said 'Mom' and 'Dad' a lot."

Nala and Marion nodded.

"I saw them," I said carefully. "They were talking." I wasn't ready to share that I'd seen baby burrito me and Aine. I knew I'd need to share this with her. But I needed time to process this for myself.

I saw. We all did, Fangorn's voice moved through my head. It was soft, and quiet. *We will talk later.*

The door closed from his side. Okay, that was weird.

Back to right now. I would have to tell Aine. I wasn't sure she was part of the *we* Fangorn was talking about. That wasn't going to happen until I managed to end the spell that kept me here. And move away from this city and all the negative things I'd experienced.

"That's amazing," Nala said. "You got all that from the stone?"

I nodded.

"May I hold it?"

I hesitated. Did I want her to see this? Then I thought about how at this point, Nala was some part of this. She was an ally. We didn't have that many.

I handed over the stone.

She cupped it in her hand and then held it between her palms. She closed her eyes and leaned back in her chair. I could tell she was breathing deeply, concentrating on the stone. Her eyes flew open.

"There's great power—really amazing amounts of it—in this stone. It's not anything I can access, however. This is obviously only for you." She carefully handed it back to me.

When my hand closed around it, I felt something. I didn't know what. But it was like a puzzle piece fell into place. What place, what piece—I had no idea.

For the first time in a long time, I didn't worry about it. I'd figure it out. I could ask the dragons. I wondered if Fangorn would tell me the truth. It wasn't that I didn't trust him because I did. He'd had plenty of opportunities to tell me the hell with my agenda and make me part of his. He hadn't.

But he wasn't being totally straight with me either. The more things went on the more I knew this was a fact.

I decided that I would just go on with my plans. If Fangorn hadn't told me something, he had his reasons. If he chose not to take me into his confidence, or plans, or whatever—then he'd get the fallout when he did tell me.

So much of my life had been spent working around the desires, needs, and whims of others. It's what I had to do in the foster system, and it's what I had to do when I worked, breaking the law, for others. This was my norm.

Not anymore. I was going to do what was best for me and the only family that was honest with me. Who'd been honest since we'd met. My mouth broke into half a grin which I quickly stifled. This wasn't the time for me laughing.

When I slid the stone into the pocket of my—my dad's—coat, something else clicked. I was supposed to have the coat, and now, the stone. I had something from both my parents. Something that had been wrong was right now. Not that I had any idea of what that something was—but it was right.

"What do we need to do to break the spell?" Margrite was focused on the task at hand.

"It's better if we do this business at night. It might look kind of weird in the middle of the day," Marion said. Her brows were creased, a sure sign that she was worried.

I reached across Margrite and squeezed Marion's hand. My touch made her jump. "I'm not thrilled you kept all this from me, but I get why you did," I said.

That wasn't just for her benefit. I did get it. Marion had always been an ally and a friend to me. There was no reason for me to think of her otherwise. I thought she was wrong to have kept all this shit from me, but she didn't have some kind of secret agenda. She was trying to do right by her friend's wishes, and what she saw.

I met Marion's eyes. Tears shimmered, and she was really trying not to cry.

"Thank you. I... I don't want things to be bad between us," she said.

Nala reached under her table and brought out the tissues. Marion took one and dabbed at her eyes.

"Can we try tonight?" Margrite brought the conversation back, not only because that was who she was, but to give Marion a little space.

I smiled at Margrite briefly. She was good like that.

Marion nodded. "We can. I'm serious when I tell you this isn't a big deal. We'll be done in five minutes once I follow the instructions."

"If it works," I said. "How come you weren't so sure when you first mentioned this?"

"I looked at it before I came back with the box. It's a lot more simple than I thought. So why wouldn't it work?" Marion asked.

"Things don't always go as planned," Nala said.

"Don't we know it," Margrite added.

I did laugh at that. She was right. That had been life for us lately.

"Would you like some assistance?" Nala asked.

Margrite looked to me. I appreciated that. I nodded. "I think that would be good."

"All right, then let's meet at 8:30 in Merchants Park."

"Why there?" Margrite asked.

"Because that's where Maria told me to go. I don't know if it's the place or just where she knew because that's where she lived, but that's what she told me. I don't want to deviate from her instructions."

That was across town, in a much nicer place than we were. Is that where my mom grew up?

"Are her parents still alive?"

"What?" Marion was surprised.

"Her parents. Are they still alive?"

"Um—no. They were after she came back, and they tried to be helpful, but your grandmother…" Marion's lips pursed, then she continued. "Your grandparents had ideas on how you should be raised, how things should go. They hadn't been all that jazzed about your dad, so their idea was to pretend he never existed, and move on from there. That went over really well," she added.

Then she grinned. "Your mom was so sick, physically and mentally, and I was with her when she told them both to piss off, that she was going to raise her kids the way she wanted. Since she only had you, they were all over her about where Aine was, and she said, I'm an adult, and you can't stop me. So, she packed up and left with me." Her eyes teared again, and she stopped to wipe them.

"She was so brave. She'd lost your dad, and Aine, and she was sick, and she was scared, but she told her parents to pound sand. She didn't need to. They would have paid for everything … and I asked her why she didn't just do that, because she wasn't at one hundred percent, and things were going to be so much harder for her now. She said she'd seen what happened when you let people take over, and I've never seen her look so angry and sad at the same time. All of those reasons were why she left," Marion sighed. "She tried so hard for a couple of years. Then she realized that she was sick, sicker than before. That's why she gave you to me. She didn't want her parents to find you, or whatever it was that your father was dealing with to catch up with you. I know you're mad at me."

I hesitated. "I wish you'd told me all this before." My anger had been fading away, but it wasn't totally gone.

"I wanted to. But I couldn't. Your grandparents are gone now. When they died, I did some discreet checking. I wanted to see if I could set you up, or if they'd left anything to her, or you. But they'd disowned your mom and gave everything to the local shelter. The animal shelter, not people," she added.

"Good to see their priorities are on point," Margrite crossed her arms and rolled her eyes. "Your mom was right, A. You've been better off without that kind of family."

I didn't disagree. But it might have been nice to have some more comfort, or security. I'd never know. Which meant I needed to put it aside.

"Okay, the park tonight. We'll meet you there," I stood up.

"Where are you going?"

"Margrite and I are going to eat. Then we're going to do the things we need to do for us. And we'll meet you guys tonight."

Walking out I felt a pang. Part of me wanted to talk to Marion, find out more about my mom. But the box under my arm would tell me some of that. And I wanted to look the papers in the box over without anyone looking over my shoulder.

Margrite caught up with me on the sidewalk. "That was kind of abrupt, don't you think?"

"I don't know what to think. But I wanted to get out."

"You're hungry again?"

"Let's go somewhere new," I said. This part of town, my part of town, was suddenly not feeling safe. I'd felt a relative measure of safety for years in the anonymity of the rundown area. But not anymore.

"All right," she shrugged. "Whatever you want."

We headed out, and I took a long way back to the motel where we were staying. Along the way, we stopped at a Mexican place. I brought the box into the restaurant with me, not wanting to let it get far away from me.

Margrite looked at me, and the box, but didn't say anything.

"Can we look in it?" Margrite indicated the box.

"Yeah, when we get back."

"Any reason why it's having lunch with us?"

"I don't feel good leaving it outside," I said.

She nodded, and we ordered. Once the waitress was gone, she leaned in.

"You think your mom was well off? That Merchants Park is in a nice part of town."

"I know. She had to be, at one time. But it doesn't matter. Cats are eating good off my inheritance," I grinned at her.

"You could be a trust fund baby and not even know it," she teased.

"I wouldn't have been able to be friends with you, or have anything that I do now," I said.

"Oh, you didn't want to give up this life?" She spread her hands out in mock disbelief.

"Sometimes, sure," I leaned back into the booth, thinking. "But it sounds like my mom didn't have a lot of freedom, and she was trying to get the hell away from that."

Her expression changed. "I'm sorry. I'm not trying to poke at your mom. I just—"

I waved a hand. "It's all right. I know. I'm starting to feel a little too serious anymore. Like, we haven't laughed in ages."

"It's been kind of a serious two weeks," Margrite said.

"Doesn't mean we have to turn into grumpy blue hairs," I said.

She looked at me, and then burst out laughing.

"What?"

When she stopped, she looked at me. "There's no way you

could be a blue hair, Aodan. No way, even if you were old and grumpy."

"I am totally missing your point."

That set her off again. I crossed my arms and rolled my eyes and looked at the other people in the restaurant. Margrite finally calmed herself.

"You done?"

"I think I am for the time being. Get over yourself, A."

"What, exactly, do I need to get over?"

"Let's talk about what we do after we break the spell tonight," she said, her tone going serious.

"Can you keep your voice down?" I hissed. "People are already more aware of you and your laughing like a demented hyena."

She snickered. "Sure, Gramps. I'll keep it down for the hordes that are milling around."

"For God's sake," I muttered.

"Seriously. What do you want to do?"

"I think we get new phones today, and once that damn spell is history, we book our flights."

Her eyes widened. "You still want to go through with all the things we planned before?"

I nodded. "Why not?"

"Uh, because everything's changed? Because it's not just you and me anymore?" She frowned at me.

"Just because things have changed doesn't change what I want for myself, for our future."

"Aodan, you're not being reasonable."

"No, what's not reasonable is expecting me to upend my whole life for something that's been part of my life for about ten seconds."

"That doesn't change the fact that it is part of your life. Running away from it won't make it go away."

Sometimes I really hated her dedication to honesty. "I'm not running away. And you don't have to come if you are so against it." I also really hated that I sounded no older than twelve.

"Don't be a dumb ass." She rolled her eyes now. "Of course, I'm coming with you. I stand with you no matter what. You know that. But that doesn't mean I won't question you when I think it's the thing to do."

"No shit," I said.

Thankfully, the food came, and this no-win conversation came to a momentary end. I knew it wasn't over. Margrite and I didn't shy away from the hard things, even though sometimes I wished she'd give it a rest.

After lunch, we made a couple of stops, getting new phones and a few more things that we needed. We'd been frugal for so long that the ability to just get things was amazing. When we got back to the motel Margrite went and laid down.

I took off my coat and laid down on the other bed. I'd pulled the stone from my mom out of my pocket and turned it over and over in my hand. What was this thing? Why did it talk to me like it had? Because it had talked. Was it like a memory stone? Did the dragons even have such a thing?

It felt like I was trying to grab onto smoke from a fire I couldn't see. There were so many things I didn't know. With my mom and dad both gone, how was I supposed to learn?

I thought about the scene I'd watched. My dad knew something. I'd seen the way he looked at baby burrito Aine and me, and he'd known something. Did dragons have psychics?

The more I thought about it, the more I thought I needed to talk to Fangorn. I'd been avoiding talking to him, and he seemed to know that because in the last couple of days, he hadn't contacted me. Until I'd seen my parents in Nala's shop. Which was good—I needed the time for me, and to get my life back in some semblance of order.

I shook my head. To sort this, I had to make the lines of what I knew and didn't know clear. Also, I wanted to figure out

who I would have to speak with to find out the things I wanted
—needed—to know.

At some point, I would also have to share the memory with
Aine. She deserved that. She'd said that she'd been raised by
Eilor. That meant she had no memory of anything else.
Certainly not our parents, or that we were loved. I couldn't
imagine that she got a lot of love or any sort of positive
emotions with the crazy guy.

Watching our parents worry over us hit me hard. It wasn't
fair that I kept that to myself. I sighed. She was able to be part
of the collective. Time to see if it worked.

8

---

*A**ine?* I sent it out into the wherever. I wanted to tell her in person, but I was impatient, and restless.

No answer.

Aine?

Yes?

It's Aodan.

I know. Are you well?

Was I? *I don't know. I wanted … I wanted to share something with you.*

What?

I was given a box of our mom's stuff.

From where?

Her friend. She left a bunch of things with her friend. There was a stone in the box, and when I touched it, I saw one of her memories.

What was it?

Even through this kind of communication, I could feel her get more excited.

Can I show you? I don't know how else to share it.

Silence, and then, *Try remembering it, and we'll see if it's shared.*

For this, I'd need to close my eyes. I gripped the stone and thought about what I'd seen before, trying to make sure that I didn't forget anything, or leave anything else.

The scene played in front of me pretty much like it had before. I didn't try to interject or communicate. I wanted Aine to see it with the purity that I had.

When the scene faded, I could feel a strong emotion coming from her. There was something else—the other dragons had seen this as well. But they were in the background. Letting Aine and I have this moment.

Is that what you remember? Her voice sounded sad.

As much as I can, yeah.

That was us.

Yeah.

Did you really call us baby burritos? What is a burrito?

It's a food. A flat bread that is rolled up and filled with meat and cheese and things.

A moment, and then I felt her laughter. *We're a rolled-up food?*

That's what it looked like to me.

Well, it's not a bad description. Why did you think Lionel—our father —she stumbled a little over calling him that--*thought you needed the stone, or whatever he was talking about?*

I shrugged as I answered. *I have no idea. The more I learn, the more I find out I don't know much at all. I feel like...*

Like what?

Like there's a lot we don't know, and maybe others do. I wanted to be careful. I knew that she and Fangorn were close, closer than I was with him.

Oh, that's nothing new. I grew up with Eilor who had plans within plans within schemes within double crosses. He was ridiculous with the amount of information he refused to share with anyone.

But he's not the guy running things. Shouldn't that withholding info change?

You mean Fangorn?

Among others. What about your husband? Brennan? Their dad?

I could almost feel Aine sigh. *They're not bad people. They don't see things from the same point of view that I, or you do. But they don't have agendas that will hurt either of us.*

Maybe not on purpose, I countered.

Another sigh. *You're not wrong. I hate to admit that, but I think there's a lot that they don't know either.*

Which also doesn't help us. Do you think Fangorn is being honest?

Why wouldn't he be?

I've felt like he's holding back.

He probably is.

She didn't sound as bothered by this as I was.

He had to hide himself a great deal over the past thousand years, she continued. *I don't think that's a habit that is easy to break.*

We're his family.

We're not his only family. Speaking of which, when are you returning?

Just what I didn't want to talk about.

I don't know, I thought.

You should come back.

I have a life here.

There was silence and then she said, *You could have one here, too.*

In that one sentence, I could feel her longing to have a relationship with her brother, and the pull of it was strong. I felt it too. But that would mean abandoning my life here. No one seemed to get that everything important here was just as much my priority as learning about the rest of my family—and that if the two came down to a choice, I would pick the family who I knew, who I had no doubts of.

That was part of the problem I had with my dragon side. That side saw no reason why I would stay in the Human Realm. They discounted my concern for Margrite. They didn't understand that she was more family than anyone else I'd met. Well, maybe that was unfair. They'd all risked a lot to help me get her away from Eilor. Maybe they didn't discount her. But they didn't see her the same way I did.

I couldn't say to them that she was the only family I'd had

for years. Not without being mean. And that right now, she was the family I put first. I couldn't tell Aine, or Fangorn these things before. Certainly not now when I could feel the wishes of my sister.

That would be at the expense of the life I already have. If I have to choose, I'm not going to abandon the only member of my family who's been with me for years, I finally responded.

I understand that. I would just like ... her words trailed off.

I know. She didn't need to explain it to me. Talking to her made me miss those in the Dragon Realm all the more. The walls I'd put up crumbled as though they'd never been there. Aine got it.

What are you doing now?

Margrite and I are meeting Mom's friend to break the spell she used that keeps me in this place.

Mother wasn't magic. Her response was quick.

Her friend said that Dad gave her some of his power—by the way, you know what he meant by the other thing? I was referring to when I'd seen him reassuring our mother.

I don't know.

Would Fangorn?

Probably.

Can we ask him?

I don't know, she said again.

This isn't helping, I said.

I am not here to make things easy. I am always going to tell you the truth.

In those two sentences, I felt a great deal about who my sister was. She told the truth regardless of the outcome. And she knew that I wanted something different but told me the truth, anyway.

I know. That doesn't mean I want to hear it.

Her amusement vibrated through our connection again. *Very few do, in spite of what people say about seeking the truth. It's an uncomfortable aspect of refusing to lie.*

I don't know about that, I thought. *You seem to enjoy it.*

Perhaps I do. Having grown up with lies stacked on lies, I will always take the truth.

I always thought I knew the truth, I responded.

I'm sorry.

It's all right. So what should I do? Talk to Fangorn?

They miss you. We all do, she said.

A wave of longing swept over me. Being with my dragon clan—family—I felt more at home, more where I ought to be, than I'd ever felt anywhere else in my life. It was the most powerful pull I'd ever felt. And I had to keep it under control. *I miss them too.*

Aine didn't respond, but she didn't have to. I knew what she thought.

All right, I thought. *I'll get in touch with him later. I have to deal with other things today.*

What spell? She changed the subject abruptly.

*Don't you remember me telling you that I couldn't leave the city? Our parents did that. One of Mom's friends—*I left out the part that she was also my caseworker—*got in touch to let me know that she could help me.*

There's a lot you're not telling me.

Story of my friggen life, I thought.

The amusement came through again. *I understand. I lived in a cloud of lies and misconceptions. You don't have to tell me everything. Not yet anyway. Good luck with the spell. Pay attention so you can share it later.*

Her presence was gone.

When I'd met Aine, she kind of irritated me. But the more I talked with her, the more I liked her. She was to the point, didn't screw around, and didn't waste time. I liked that a great deal.

Add Fangorn to the list of people I needed to talk to, things I needed to deal with. He knew about the memory. The question was, exactly what did he know about it?

But first, time to deal with Marion and my parents good but misguided intentions.

When it was time to go, the butterflies that showed up before a job woke up and had a field day in my stomach. I could feel sweat on the back of my neck. The worst that could happen was that I wouldn't be able to leave. That didn't sound bad, but it was so shitty for all the things we had planned that I couldn't even go there. Not right now.

"Ready?" Margrite appeared next to me.

"Yeah, let's get this over with."

We rode out to where we'd agreed to meet Marion. She and Nala pulled up in Marion's small dark sedan ten minutes after we'd parked the bike under some trees.

The sky flared multi-colored, with pinks and blues mixed in with the gold of the setting sun. It was gorgeous. I didn't often get to sit out in a park and watch the sun. I shoved my hands in my pockets, enjoying the sight. It smelled different up here, away from the city proper. It smelled good.

"This is a good sign," Margrite said. She'd moved up to stand beside me.

She was always so quiet. It was her skill as a thief. She just had a harder time getting the whatever she was stealing. But the getting to it undetected? No one was better, not even me.

"I hope so."

"Hope what?" Nala came behind us.

"That this—" Margrite indicated the sunset— "Bodes well for what we're about to do."

"Do you anticipate problems?" Nala sounded surprised.

"You don't?" I asked.

She shrugged. "This seems simple. It's much harder to set a spell than to remove it."

"Yeah, but this has conditions," I objected.

"All magic does. There are always things that have to be in place for it to happen."

I shook my head. Her reasoning didn't make sense to me. Both were tasks—but I wasn't any sort of expert on magic or the woo woo arts, so I wasn't going to argue. I just hoped that her confidence would bear out the situation. I was also

Marion stopped beside Nala. "When it gets dark, we'll do this. The sign for the city limit is there," she pointed, "So let's walk a line and go into the trees a little."

"Why?" I asked. "You said this was simple."

"It is. Or, it should be. But I don't know what's going to happen," Marion had already turned away and was heading for the city sign. Once she got there, she faced us, and then started walking into the trees. "I'd rather not have all our business out on the road, if you don't mind."

She was still a little pissed at me. Shit. I didn't want that, but I wasn't sure how to fix it.

"You're going to need to talk to her," Margrite whispered as we walked up a small rise where the trees were more numerous.

"I know," I whispered back. "I screwed up. But I don't know what to say."

Margrite made an impatient noise. "Oh, I don't know. How about the truth?"

I looked over to see her rolling her eyes.

"This isn't rocket science, A. It's really not. Just be honest."

"And say what?" I stopped.

"Whatever the truth is," she kept going, not waiting for me to answer.

"Thanks," I called. "Lots of help with that nugget."

"You get what you get," she said over her shoulder.

Shit. Be honest? I didn't even know what I thought.

"How about here?" Nala asked. She'd stopped about ten feet ahead of me.

Even though the road was not that far off, it was quieter here. Marion stopped and set down the bag she'd been carrying.

"What, we have a ceremony?" I watched as she pulled a couple of things out of it. I couldn't tell what they were as it was darker here in the trees.

"I have to say things in order. I don't want you turning into a frog, or whatever," Marion said.

She wasn't smiling.

"Yeah, not on my list either. What do you need help with?" I asked her.

"Nothing. Let me get through my instructions." She was cool.

She pulled a piece of paper from her pocket. It was old, and it had been folded and unfolded many times.

"I made your mom write it down for me and then I wrote it out based on how it sounds, because I would never remember this twenty years later. So, bear with me."

I nodded.

She said the words slowly, and carefully. They weren't English, or any language I recognized. It seemed like it took a long time. Then she looked up at me. "It's done."

"That's it?" Margrite asked.

"I told you it wouldn't take long. That's what your mom said." Marion shrugged. "There's no reason she would have lied to me."

"With everything, it feels like it should be a bigger deal," Margrite shot a look at me.

"It does. This feels too simple."

"Why don't you try and cross the boundary line?" Nala suggested.

Well, okay. Duh.

I didn't say anything but walked back the way we'd came to the city limits sign. Taking a breath, preparing myself to be shot backwards on my ass, I stepped past it. Then I took another step.

Nothing happened.

"It worked!" Margrite came up to me, a smile on her face.

That didn't happen often.

"It did," I smiled as I looked down at her. "This is it. We can leave."

"Where are you going?" Marion was behind me.

"Margrite and I have always planned to leave. So we're leaving."

"Right now?" Marion looked like she might cry. Her cool facade was gone.

"Yes. Before something else stops us."

"I want to come with you, make sure you'll be safe."

"No. No one can know where we are." I wanted away from here, away from where everyone knew Aodan and Margrite. Away from where we were a target.

"But—"

"We can call you, talk online," Margrite interrupted. "We really do need to leave."

"What have you gotten yourselves into?" Nala asked.

I rolled my eyes even though I wasn't sure she could see me with the sun disappearing on the horizon. "The life of a thief. We got to something someone else wanted." It was my turn to shrug. "We were never going to stay here."

Marion grabbed me and hugged me, hard. "I'm going to miss you. I do want to come and see you, when you think it's safe. I can't lose you entirely, Aodan."

All my anger at her faded. I'd miss her, too. She'd looked after me first, even if I didn't know it, then Margrite. She did what she promised my mom she'd do. She did the best she could with all the restrictions her job placed on her. She was family, too. Before she'd tracked us down through Nala, she was one of the people I considered family. But she couldn't come with us. That would put her in danger. At least, right now it would.

I sighed. To keep on being pissed was stupid on my part. I mean, I could continue with it. But it was stupid. I wrapped my arms around her. "Thank you," I said.

"She—they'd be so proud of you," she whispered into my shoulder.

It took everything I had not to cry like Margrite watching The Host. It was the one movie she bought and carried around with us everywhere. She-and I—had seen it a million times, and she always bawled at the end.

"I hope so," I said.

"They would. I know it. I'm proud of you. Go through the box. She left a record, as much as she could."

I nodded. I couldn't speak.

"Well, all right. How about some pie? I could use some dessert." Margrite said. "Then Aodan and I have some things to do."

"When will you leave?" Nala asked.

"Soon," I said.

"You can't leave without saying goodbye. Call me, and we'll spend time together," Marion said, releasing me.

"I will."

"I'll tell you anything you want to know," she added. "I've added to the box, with memories and things I thought she'd like me to share with you."

I felt a lump in my throat that was so large it hurt. This was a gift not only to me, but to Aine. I'd have to share this with her, too.

"That's amazing. Especially considering Aodan has been kind of an ass. But it's been a rough week or so, in his defense. And you know I give him no extra credit." Margrite was right there with the right words.

Even though she sounded snarky, I knew she was taking up for me. She could tell that I was overcome with emotion.

Marion smiled at us. "You ready?" She asked Nala.

Nala nodded. She touched me on the arm and gave Margrite a hug. "Come see me before you go," she said.

Then the two women walked away. I saw Nala put her arm around Marion, and Marion didn't shrug her off.

"Wow," Margrite said. "That was… intense."

"You think?"

"More than I thought. You are an ass, and she really does love you."

"I know." I was an ass.

"Well, ass, let's get home. Our temporary home," she amended. "We need to see what we can schedule, and how we can get the hell out of here." Margrite sounded crisp and business-like.

I appreciated it. I needed a moment to pull myself together. I tucked the box under my arm as we walked back to where we parked the bike. I saw Marion and Nala driving away, and both women waved as they went past us.

"I'm going to miss her," Margrite said, watching the car disappear into the night.

"We don't have to go," I began.

"Are you crazy? Yes, we have to go! We have Caleb on our ass, and sooner or later, Luke is going to spill the beans on exactly how much we made off that last job. He can't keep that to himself forever. Not to mention Caleb will go ape shit when he hears it, but every loser within a ten-mile radius is going to be planning on how to get the money from us. I'm sure half of them think we keep it under our bed, so we'll never be safe anywhere. No, A, we have to leave. If I'm sure of anything, that's it."

"I agree, so you're getting no argument from me. I just don't want you to feel that you have to do anything."

"I don't," she said, taking the box from me. "I want to get out of here. I love you, seriously, but this place hasn't exactly been a bastion for the warm and fuzzy memories."

"That's true," I agreed. "All right, let's get back to the room, and we'll plan the escape route."

I grinned at her, and she gave me one of her rare smiles in answer. Margrite is shorter than I am, and has short, dark hair. She dresses in a lot of black, although recently she's taken to wearing flannel shirts over whatever else she's wearing. She reminded me of Aine—small, dark, and capable. I'd heard guys say she was beautiful, but I'd never thought about it. She was just Margrite, and the best friend I'd ever had.

We headed back to the motel room and spent the rest of the night booking flights. We stuck to our original plan—island hop using different names so that by the time we reached our final destination, Aodan and Margrite weren't as traceable. I didn't think we'd entirely disappear, but we'd do a decent job of it.

We planned to leave two days from now. Margrite wanted a day to say goodbye, although with just Nala, I wasn't sure what the holdup was. But I didn't argue. We also needed to head down to Washington, D.C., because we were flying out of Dulles.

As we went to bed that night, I felt better than I had in a long time. Even though I hadn't opened the box, I'd packed it carefully into my backpack, so that it wouldn't leave my side. When we got to Grand Turk, which was our final stop, we'd be moving into a cottage that I'd found for sale. I'd been talking to the real estate agent via email before I'd been dragged into dragon affairs.

It was amazing how easy it was to buy the place. Money helped with making things easy. House of the Sun was the name of it, and while it sounded rather grand, it was a little old cottage that looked right out onto the water. We both loved it. It wasn't big, but it would be ours, and I didn't have to jerry-rig a thing.

All of which made it perfect.

We just had to get there.

I closed my eyes. Only a few more days.

9

*T*he night air felt wonderful on my face, and I could feel the shifts of the wind as I flew. Closing my eyes momentarily, I inhaled the night.

I felt a gust beneath my left wing, and I shifted to take advantage of the change. The world below me was small, and the lights of the world twinkled like stars.

Here in the clouds, it was calm and quiet.

The clouds? The clouds? What—I looked around.

I was awake, and I was flying.

What the hell? I yelled in my head. *You can't just go out on your own!*

Aodan? Are you all right?

No! My dragon decided to take a nighttime stroll!

I don't understand.

Fangorn, I am flying. In the Human Realm. I have no idea how I got here.

Try not to hit anything, his voice was dry.

That is not very helpful.

What do you want me to say?

What do I do?

Land? Shift?

Holy hell. He really didn't see the problem here.

You cannot keep your dragon caged, Aodan.

Be quiet. I need to manage this without an audience. I slammed the door in my head shut. No one needed to see this if it all went badly.

We need to land, I said to my dragon.

I could tell he wanted to fly longer.

I don't even know where we are.

There was a smug feeling that came as a response. He'd flown us out like this so I had to let him fly.

All right. Let's make a U-turn, and head back to where we started. I won't complain at all.

No response from him.

Come on, man.

My right wing kicked up, and I wheeled in the sky, making a graceful arc as I turned back. I could feel his sadness, and resignation, and I felt like the worst kind of jerk.

When we get to the island, we can fly all we want, I thought.

The feeling of sadness didn't leave. The beauty of being out tonight, flying, was gone. Me and my dragon were both unhappy.

I didn't know how to fix this.

Finally, the lights of the city that I recognized came into view.

How did you make it out undetected? I thought.

No answer.

The motel came into view, and I circled above it, looking to see if there were any stray people in the area that might see me and cause some kind of fuss. There was no one. I landed in the vacant lot behind the motel, and after taking a few steps, shifted.

I felt amazing and terrible all at once.

"I'm sorry," I said. I stood still, listening. No one seemed to have heard or seen anything. Carefully, I walked back to the room. The door was unlocked, and the light from the parking lot shone in on the bed where Margrite was sleeping. She stirred, but didn't wake.

I crept into bed, and willed myself not to think.

I woke up to a pounding on the door so loud that it startled me. In trying to get up quickly, I nearly fell out of the bed.

Margrite was sitting up in her bed, the blankets clutched up around her. "What the hell?" She asked.

"I don't know."

"Makes you wish we had a gun, huh?"

"One of the few times," I glared at her as I pulled on pants. I went to the door and put my eye up to the peephole.

"Oh, shit."

"What?"

"It's Stefan," I said.

"Oh, shit," Margrite echoed me.

"Forget it," I said. "Let's just face this. If he gets out of hand, I'll go dragon on him, and fry him to a crisp." I was tired of running and hiding. We'd been hired for a job. We'd done it. If that meant I beat his guy out, too damn bad. Besides, I thought it might make my dragon happier to beat a little bad guy ass.

I already knew I could make Caleb piss himself. While Stefan was Eilor's brother, he didn't seem to be on good terms with Eilor. So while Eilor was out there, still being a damn problem, I thought I could handle this.

I hoped. I hoped it wasn't just anger pushing me. With that happy thought, I yanked open the door.

"What?"

Stefan held up his hands. I could see a black SUV parked behind the cars in front of the door, and a couple of guys standing around it, waiting.

Caleb was noticeably absent. The thought made me grin.

"I am not trying to hurt you." He shook his empty hands. "If you'll give me a chance, I just want to talk."

"Alone. And if you try any magic shit, I'll take care of it." I glared.

He looked over his shoulder. "Keep your voice down, please."

He had the same way of speaking as Eilor, and it made all the hair on my neck stand up.

Then he turned back. "They don't know. I've managed to ease the fears—and memories--of those who were with me that night, but they don't need any more information than that."

"What do you want?"

"May I come in? I don't want to discuss this in the parking lot." There was the snotty Realm guy again.

It must be a family trait. No wonder they weren't friends.

"Hold on," I closed the door and looked at Margrite. "What do you want to do?"

She was up and pulling on clothes. "Let him in. Only him. If he does anything, fry him. We'll pull the fire alarm as we leave."

"You're the best," I grinned at her. "Seriously."

She grinned back. "Don't you forget it."

I yanked the door open again. "You can come in."

Stefan stepped in, and then I shut the door behind him quickly, locking it.

"Worried?" He asked.

"Shouldn't I be?"

"I don't know."

"Don't be cute," I said. "Sit down." I gestured to the chair and table by the window. "Start talking and don't make a meal of it. We don't have all day."

Slowly, keeping his hands out of his pockets, Stefan lowered himself into the chair.

"So. Were you the dragon?"

"I'm not the subject of our conversation. You wanted to talk, so talk," I crossed my arms, standing away from him. I wanted room to shift if I needed it.

Stefan sighed. "All right. Let me ask you this—what is your relationship with my brother?"

"Eilor? Aren't you two all hunky dory?" Margrite asked.

"No. Not even close."

"I understand you were banished from the Realms," I said. I knew why. I wanted to see what he would say.

"I was. But the thing I was accused of—I didn't do it."

"Yeah, it was the guy next to you," I rolled my eyes.

His brows lowered, and he inhaled deeply. I recognized the signs of someone trying to keep their temper in check. "If you're a dragon, you need to stay the hell away from Eilor. He will use you, and when he's done, he will kill you. That's what he does." Stefan leaned back in the chair. The look on his face suggested he wasn't seeing us, but something else entirely.

"I was thrilled when we won the Dragon Wars. You have no idea how frightening they were, the kind of damage they did. Not that the fae were any less capable of intense damage—" he smiled sadly. "But when it was over, we were able to get on with the business of healing."

"Easy to do when most of the dragons were dead," I said quietly.

"Yes, it was. Most of the dragons weren't willing to concede, to try and live in peace. They were angry, and they didn't want to surrender. They gave everyone else within the Realms no choice! I didn't want to kill them, but if they weren't going to honor a peace, then yes, they needed to die! The only way they would have stopped was if the rest of the races of the Realms were gone!" His voice rose, and he leaned forward.

"But not all of them died, and I was pleased when my brother was chosen not only as the king of the Dragon Realm, but the guardian of the dragons. For the next hundred years, things were peaceful, and life was restored to something like it had been prior to the war."

"If you weren't a dragon," I said.

"Yes, if you weren't a dragon. But if you make war, you

must be prepared for the consequences. Whatever else one might say about those dragons long ago, they didn't shy from the truth, or the outcome of their actions." A look I couldn't decipher crossed his face. It was almost sad.

Weird. He was so proud of nearly wiping the dragons out. Why would he have anything to be sad about?

"You admire them?" Margrite didn't sound as hostile.

"A being who will die for their principles? Yes. Of course."

"But you were fine with them dying." She crossed her arms.

"You make a choice. Then you live with the outcome of that choice. It's sad, for the dragons were magnificent, but they were determined to end all other life that didn't agree to their terms." He shrugged. "Survival isn't always pretty, young lady."

"What do you want?" I was tired of hearing about how the few dragons I'd met didn't deserve to live.

"I want to know what happened to the box that you stole from my employee."

I burst out laughing. He sounded so prim, so proper. "Your employee?"

Even Margrite chuckled.

"My associate, if you wish."

"I don't discuss my work with anyone other than the people who hire me," I said. "And I have no idea what you're talking about."

Now it was Stefan's turn to smile. "Let us not be coy, Mr. George. You stole the box from Caleb. I was unaware that…" he considered his next words. "That another party had an equally motivated interest in the item. But since they did, I want to know where you delivered it."

I held up a hand. "Whoa, buddy. Since we're in a similar sort of business, you know that people like me have no idea where the fruits of our labors end up."

Margrite burst out laughing at that. Stefan and I both looked at her. When she finished, she looked at him. "I think you're probably nothing but bad news, but when you make Aodan clean up his language, you might not be all bad."

"Thanks," I said, rolling my eyes.

Stefan laughed. "You two are a good team. I could only wish that I had a team like you. Would you—"

"Don't even finish that sentence," I said. "You employ Caleb. He's a complete—"

"Moron," Margrite said. "And while it's nice to see he's scared shitless of you, you've kept him in your employ. Don't bother. It's a waste of everyone's time. It's clear you don't want anyone with a brain to work for you."

Stefan crossed his arms. "Very good, Miss Duchamps. Well, it was worth a try. But back to the box. I need it."

"Why?" I asked.

"Because I want to go home."

"So you can unleash another Eilor on the Realms? I think they've got enough problems," I said.

"Is that what you think? Well, it makes sense," he said. "My reputation was sealed the moment my brother embarked on his great ambition. When we were young," he leaned back in his chair.

"We don't care," Margrite said.

"Oh, but you should. It bears into what is happening right now, why Eilor is desperately seeking you and your talents at this moment," Stefan gave me a nod.

"Go on," I said. I ignored the noise of protest from Margrite.

"When we were young, we saw a dragon kill a man from our town. It was a punishment for something he'd done, and it was probably deserved. The fae didn't dole out death by dragon often. But it was horrific. We were in town that day, and Eilor saw it. I was somewhere with our mother, but he and our father watched it. From that day onward, Eilor was different."

He sighed. "He saw the dragons as a threat to not only the fae, but all the Realms. They were the strongest creatures physically, and their magic had no match. I've seen the dragons at war, and it was truly frightening."

"You were around for the war I keep hearing about?" I asked. I didn't trust this joker any further than I could throw him, but I was interested despite that.

Stefan nodded. "Coupled with what Eilor saw when he was a child, I understand where his motivation stems from."

"I don't," I said, crossing my arms. "How many people, how many dragons, have died for his unresolved issues?"

"Childhood trauma is no excuse for being an asshole," Margrite added.

"No, it's not. But understanding those you stand against is important," Stefan said.

I'd noticed with Eilor that when I swore, he got irritated. Stefan didn't even blink when Margrite swore at him. He must have been here for a long time.

"How long have you lived in the Human Realm?" I asked.

"A long time. There is much that I admire about the beings in this Realm, but I want to go home. While I've been gone a long time, I doubt the Fae Realms have changed so much. Life is slower there. There is more time for everything. This world has become too fast, and I don't want to be here anymore."

"What do you want from us?" Margrite asked.

"I want your help to go home."

"Hey, that's your problem," I said. "Whatever you have to solve with the king or whatever—that's on you. I can't help you there."

"Oh, but I think you can." Stefan smiled.

I didn't like the smile at all. It reminded me too much of his brother.

Margrite moved away from me. It took me a second to figure out what the hell she was doing. Oh. She was giving me room to shift.

I focused on my dragon. He was stirring. He felt the threat in Stefan's words. I could also feel his—my—yearning to be out, to stretch and be free. I'd only shifted the one time since I'd come back from the Dragon Realm, and he was feeling stifled. And that hadn't been something we'd agreed on.

It's okay. No matter what, we'll head out tonight. Then we're in the islands, and it's all open ocean.

I felt his acquiescence as well as his grumble. It was weird. We were one and the same, but the dragon had his own voice. It was my voice, but my dragon brain. Maybe that's how I needed to think of it—as my dragon brain. I had a human, and I guess fae, brain. I also had a piece of that brain that was all dragon.

And the dragon wanted to kick Stefan's smug ass.

Hold on, I told the dragon. *Let's see what else he wants to say.*

Not the best idea, I heard.

No! Fangorn, let me handle this!

I am unsure you can. He is an evil being.

Yeah, we have a special on those, I thought.

I do not understand.

Stop! Let me focus!

Thankfully, he shut up. I looked at Stefan, who was watching me with a small smile. It was smug. Yeah, the dragon had the right idea, but I knew I needed to hear whatever it was he thought he had that we'd want.

"Why is that?"

"Because I can trade your efforts for information."

Margrite snorted, making sure it was loud and unmistakable. "Information isn't a sure thing."

Stefan steepled his fingers. "You are absolutely correct, Margrite. But there are times when the value of the information offered is visible to anyone who hears of it."

"Oh, you have a treasure chest?" I asked. "Not interested. Margrite and I have no interest in anything about the Dragon Realm. We're done there."

Stefan laughed. "You're good, Aodan, but you're lying your ass off."

"Nope. Think what you like."

"What's your info?" Margrite glared at him.

"I can give you Eilor."

"Bullshit," she said.

"You aren't from there. You've been there once, am I correct? Under duress, as well. How would you know, if you'll excuse my bluntness?"

Stefan was a mix of the guys I knew and Fangorn. I didn't like relating him to someone I cared for, but that was what his manner reminded me of.

"Because everyone over there is looking for his ass, and they haven't found him. They live there. They haven't had a long absence," she added pointedly.

There are times when I get a stark reminder of why Margrite and I are best friends. This conversation was one of them. Stefan could kill her easily, I was sure. I knew that the time she'd spent with Eilor had left a mark on her. She had to feel the power coming off him. I could have felt that even without my dragon awareness.

But she didn't back down or give any quarter.

"It's a shame that humans cannot often survive in the Realms. You are a fierce warrior," Stefan said.

Shit. We were even thinking along the same lines. I didn't like that at all.

"However, you are incorrect. I grew up with Eilor. We grew up in the Dragon Realm, and unlike how he is now, he was not always a king. We were children from a family that didn't have much. It meant we were resourceful and careful. Why is it, do you think, that no one from the Realms has caught him yet?"

"How do you know all this?" I asked.

"I have … contacts that keep me apprised of happenings in my home." His face closed a little.

That was interesting. Contacts? That was something to note, and see if we could find out who that was. And something to tell Fangorn.

You hearing this? I thought out to the collective.

I stopped myself. This was a red herring. In spite of the emotional reaction he'd given, there were tons of people that could be chatting with him. Or no one at all.

"Ok. Why can't anyone find him?"

"What do you think boys do all day? They explore. We know the Dragon Realm like few others. That's always been something that his enemies underestimated."

"How do we know you're telling the truth?"

"You help me return to the Realm, and I'll take you, or whomever you wish me to take, to every single hiding place I can think of."

"Yeah, let's just walk right into that trap." Margrite rolled her eyes.

"I'm with her," I said. "What do we look like, stupid?"

"Take it or leave it. This is a one-time offer, and it's not available for long."

I risked a glance at Margrite, knowing that he was watching.

Stefan got up abruptly, and I tensed, willing my dragon to come out if I needed him.

"I will leave you to discuss or confer with one another, or anyone else you need to speak with. I'll be here tomorrow morning."

"You're assuming that goes along with our plans." I didn't like his ordering us around.

"You can spare one day for whatever it is you have planned to address this." He shrugged. "Or not. It's up to you. I will return to the Realms one way or the other. But it's on your head whether I offer assistance. Should you spurn my offer, I will do nothing to help you and yours in the fight against my brother."

"Nothing like a little blackmail," Margrite said.

"Exactly. I am glad you understand the situation," Stefan smiled at her and walked out the door, shutting it behind him.

Margrite sprang forward, locking it. Then she turned and leaned against it. "That guy is a creep."

"He is, but he's not entirely wrong."

"He's like every other creep out here. He'll only help if he gets what he wants."

I laughed. "Are we any different?"

She opened her mouth to reply, and then closed it. "I don't know. Don't go all moral on me when I want to be pissed."

"I was hoping to get the hell out of here without checking in with my … you know," I said. After my dragon's nighttime run, and the fact I needed to talk to Fangorn about my mom's memory … I was in serious avoidance mode.

"Why? Are you afraid they'll try and stop you?"

After a moment, I nodded.

"Why would he do that? He wants you to be happy."

"He wants me back in the Dragon Realm."

"That's not such a bad thing, Aodan."

"We've been over this. Let's book our flights, and then leave. We can talk to pain in our ass tomorrow, and then we're leaving. No ifs, ands, or buts. I'm done with delays."

We spent the next hour finalizing our plans. I suppose I should be grateful that Stefan showed up before we bought the non-refundable tickets.

After we'd finished planning the final leg, the one that would take us to Grand Turk, Margrite leaned back on her bed and looked at me. "You need to talk to him. I think the fact that he didn't check in was amazing."

10

I sighed. "He did. He felt it when Stefan was here." I wasn't going to get into the details, or that he'd seen the memory.

"Then you need to update him. Otherwise," she held up a hand, forestalling whatever she thought I would say, "He'll show up here and send all our plans right to hell."

"You're right."

I leaned back and closed my eyes. *He's gone*, I thought.

He's been with you this entire time?

No. Margrite and I had other things to do. I waited to talk with you until I knew that I could do it without a lot of interruption.

What did he want?

He wants back in the Realms. He says Eilor framed him. He wanted the box I stole because it would let him go home. He said if I, or we, or whomever, gets him home, he'll take us to all the places he knew that Eilor used to hide out in.

What could he possibly know? He's been gone for centuries.

That's along the lines of what I said. But he said they grew up in the Dragon Realm, and all they did as kids was hang outside. Like wild kids, I guess.

I haven't heard this about Eilor.

I could hear the thoughtfulness in Fangorn's words.

Yeah, well, he said there's a reason Eilor kept his history kind of secret.

That is a convenient answer.

He had one for everything. Here's the kicker, though. He said this is a one-time offer. That if we don't help him go home, when he does get home, and he's confident he will, he won't lift a hand to help us if we're still looking for Eilor.

There is the Stefan I expected.

Well, he's been here as a crime lord forever. So it rubs off on you. I couldn't understand why I was taking up for the guy at all. My dragon side still wanted to kick his ass.

Hmmphhf.

I stifled a laugh. That was a disgruntled sound if I'd ever heard it.

Then I could feel Fangorn sigh. *Oh, very well. See if you can make an agreement with him. Tell him you expect him to swear on the blood as his bond.*

What the hell does that mean? It sounds gross.

It means he must say the words, I swear, with my blood as my bond, and then whatever it is he agrees to swear. You will see nothing, but you will feel the strength of the oath. Do it in front of Margrite. I assume she's with you?

Of course.

You did not let me know that you'd found her.

I felt guilty. I'd been focused on finding Margrite, and then the whole thing with Marion—I'd forgotten to update him.

I'm sorry. It's been … hectic.

You can tell me anything. Anything, Aodan. We are your family no matter what.

I want to believe that, I thought. *I really do. It's hard.*

I could practically feel his sigh.

That is something that I can understand. Your upbringing has not inspired you to trust anyone. And we have not known one another very long.

You can trust me. I hope that at some point you will feel you can confide in me.

Great. Now I felt like an even bigger jerk. *I know this in my head, but I…*

Haven't taken it as my bond?

Something like that, but I'm not trying to offend you, I added.

You do not offend me. If anything, I am sad, and wonder if I could be doing more to allow you to trust me, to trust us all.

We're not always on the same page, Fangorn, I thought.

No, but what you want is something I will always support.

It was like there was a knife right in my heart, and his words kept twisting it.

I want to believe that, I finally thought. *But I have to stop getting distracted. Another thing we can talk about later. He'll be here soon.* More like later, but I didn't want to get into our plans.

Make him swear the blood bond.

Okay, okay.

I will tell you what to say, and he must say it as I tell you. Do you think he'll do that?

I think if he wants to get the hell out of here, he'll do what he's told.

He's old, Aodan, and he is skilled. Perhaps not as his brother, but he is not a man to be dismissed.

Oh, I don't dismiss him.

When do you see him again?

Tomorrow morning.

I will come to you once he's agreed.

All right.

Then, you will come here.

I don't know—I began.

No, you will. We have many things we must speak of. The list of things we need to speak about is getting longer.

Practically by the minute, I added.

What will Margrite do?

He was going to keep up the pretense that I was going to just dump her. Well, if he wanted to ignore it, I could ignore him too. I didn't want to argue. *We are making plans to leave.*

The spell is broken?

Yes. My mother's friend was able to break it.

Another item to add to the list.

Yeah, probably.

Plan carefully. You want to keep her safe.

Yes, I do.

Let me know when he arrives. I'll come once he's sworn. And don't shut us out. We need to be able to hear, in case he leads you to a trap.

Got it.

He didn't speak again, and I knew he'd stepped away, as it were.

"What did he say?"

"He told me to get us safely away from here."

"You told him the spell was broken?"

I nodded. "Yeah. Another thing for us to speak of," I imitated Fangorn's solemn way of speaking.

She laughed. "He means well. You know it. Stop being a big baby boo."

I laughed with her. That's exactly how I felt with my grandfather at times—like a little kid, who wanted to kick up a fuss just because.

"Well, now that Weird-n-Creepy junior is gone, let's get on with the rest of our day."

We'd planned to see Nala and Marion today. I wasn't looking forward to it. I knew it would be tough.

"Fangorn said to get Stefan to swear some bond, and then he'd come and deal with him."

"Good," Margrite got up, heading for the bathroom. "He's not as bad as Eilor, but I can totally see how he kept all the goon squads peeing their pants. He's scary."

"He is. But he isn't a dragon." I grinned.

"Kind of nice having one of those on your side." She smiled, and shut the bathroom door behind her.

A little over an hour later, we were walking into Nala's shop. There was a customer browsing the books in the back corner. Nala looked up as the bell on the door rang, and her face widened into a smile. "I'm so glad you're here!"

"I told you I would be," Margrite returned the smile.

"Come on back, darlin', I have some things for you." Nala came from around the counter and put her arm around Margrite's shoulders. "And you too, skeptical man."

I followed the two of them back behind the curtain.

"Marion told me a bit more yesterday. I don't think she told me everything, and I really don't want to know. I don't want to know where you're going, either. But you keep my number, and you call me when you get there," Nala said. "Even though I don't have all the details, I made up a bundle for you, and I have some stones, too."

"Nala, you didn't have to do that!" Margrite sounded delighted.

Nala bustled toward the shelves along the wall, pulling out a couple of small bags that she handed to Margrite. "I wrote down all the info you'll need to know."

"Thank you," Margrite pulled the other woman in close for a hug.

"I'm going to miss you, girl," Nala said.

Margrite stepped back. "Come and visit, when things are calmer."

"I will."

People say that kind of thing all the time. But I could tell that in her words, Nala would come and see us. I smiled.

"I have something for you, too, skeptic," Nala said. She went to the table where she'd read my cards, and reached underneath, pulling out a worn basket with bundles of cards in it.

Oh, no.

She took one off the top that was tied like an old-time

package with gold twine, or something like that. Handing it across to me, she said, "You need to have this. I don't know why, but after I did your reading, it wouldn't work for anyone else. I had three different customers pick it, and the cards kept exploding right out of my hand. It took me a while, but I figured out that it's your deck."

It was the dragon cards she'd read for me. "Oh, no, I can't take these. They're yours."

"They used to be. They're yours now."

"What am I—" an elbow in my back cut off the rest of my sentence. "Thank you," I finished.

Nala laughed. "I know you're not into this, and you are probably appalled. But I listen to the decks I have, and this one wanted no more of anyone else after you. It's no good for me. Not anymore."

I took them, wondering what the hell I was going to do with them.

"I also have some teas for you," Nala said.

"That would be fantastic! I'm going to miss our tea," Margrite said.

They moved into another room behind this one, behind another curtain, and their voices lowered to a murmur, a hum. I sat down at the reading table and studied the cards. Why did they make Nala think they were broken? And had to come to me? Holding them, even though I'd never admit it, I could feel some current within them.

This was the last thing I wanted. But I didn't see any way out of it.

I stuck the cards in my coat pocket and thought about all the things I'd need to talk to Fangorn about. He was right. The list was growing faster and faster. When would we ever have time?

When Eilor was dead.

The thought came to me unbidden, but it was the right answer. Nothing could really happen, life couldn't really go on, until this joker was dead. It was that simple. I wanted to be the one to kill him, but when it came to it, could I?

I was contemplating such an idea when Nala and Margrite came back in. Margrite had a plastic bag full of what looked like dirt in smaller bags.

Nala hugged her again. "I'm really going to miss you."

They stood, and it was one of those things I knew would be a memory I could always see. The sun came into the room from a small window on the far wall, and the love between them was almost a physical thing.

It occurred to me this might be something like a mom for Margrite. She'd never known her mom, and while Tina, and then Marion were nothing but good to her, they'd come to her by way of me. Nala was someone Margrite had built a relationship with all on her own.

Nala let her go, and I could see her face was wet with tears.

"You need to go. Both you go and see Marion."

Margrite nodded.

Nala looked at me. "You got the deck? You're not trying to leave it behind, are you?"

I stood up. "It's right here," I patted my pocket. "I'm not sure what I'll do with it, but it's coming home with me." I could have bitten my tongue off. Why had I said that?

"Good. Don't lose it along the way."

I nodded, and Nala came to me, embracing me. She smelled of herbs, and sunlight. I'd never noticed it before.

"All right, you two. Go. See Marion, and then get safe. And call me!" She shook her finger at Margrite.

Margrite nodded, gave her one more hug, murmuring something I couldn't hear, and then turned and walked out of the curtain into the front of the store.

"Thank you," I said, although I wasn't sure what I was thanking her for. It seemed the right thing to say. Plus, it was all awkward with Margrite tromping out like that.

"Always. Get going. You take care of her," she added.

"I will." I followed Margrite out, and when I pushed aside the curtain, I could see she was already at the front door.

11

*H*urrying, I caught up with her as she strode out onto the sidewalk, head down.

"Let's go over and see Marion," I said. I wasn't going to talk about Nala unless Margrite brought it up. That's how we'd always been. Giving each other the space to process, or to try and ignore, or whatever.

She nodded. We got on the bike and headed for the CPS office that Marion was based out of.

"I hope she's here," I said as we parked. I hated this building. It was where I'd met most of my crap foster parents. Until Tina. Miss you, I sent a thought up to wherever she might be. Love you.

When we walked in, the secretary said she was there, and she dismissed us as she picked up the phone to call Marion. We both took a seat, waiting.

The fear smell was so strong in here, it nearly made me sick. So much fear in such a contained area.

Marion came out, her heels clacking on the tiled floor. "I'm glad you two could make it. Come back to my office. Penny," she spoke to the secretary, "We will need a little time. I need to go over some of the court files with Mr. George."

Penny nodded. "I'll hold any calls."

"Thank you," Marion smiled at her as she led us back to her office.

No one spoke until we got in and she shut the door. "I've told my supervisor you wanted to go over some of the court records surrounding your inheritance and emancipation, so I've bought us some time."

"Good thinking," Margrite said. "Everyone will allow for a little CYA."

Marion laughed, and then her laugh died as she looked at me. "You are really leaving."

I sat down at the worn table that had been in her office for as long as I could remember. Even the same carvings were there. I ran my fingers over *Ya Mutha Sux* as I said, "We are. We have to."

"Will you call me?"

"Yes," Margrite answered for us both. "It may be a while, but we'll text when we get to where we're going. And then once things are calm."

It was almost word for word what she'd said to Nala. I wondered if she'd practiced it.

Marion looked at us and then turned to her desk, reaching into her purse. "Here," she handed us two small phones. "Call me when you can. When it's safer, toss these."

"Why'd you get these?" I took the one she held out to me.

"I talked with Nala a little on the way home. She told me some of the gossip on the street. You guys hit something big. People are talking."

"What a surprise," Margrite looked at me.

"Luke," I said.

"He can't keep his mouth shut. Not on a score like this."

"Will you be able to hide?" Marion asked.

"Yes," I said.

"Then go and hide. But you must stay here for a little longer. So that your visit looks legitimate." Her eyes showed me how worried she was.

That worried me more than anything. Marion was the epitome of calm. We talked of Tina, and of my mother, and after thirty-five minutes, Marion said, "I think it's safe. When are you leaving?"

"Tomorrow, by lunch."

"Good. Be safe, Aodan. I——" she stopped. "I love you."

She'd never said it before. She couldn't. I knew that. But she always had, and I knew that too.

"I love you, too," I said, and hugged her.

We stood for a bit, and then she stepped away, wiping her eyes. She hugged Margrite, and then straightened up. Opening the door, she said, "You need to go to the courthouse now, Mr. George. There's nothing else I can tell you."

"Bye," I whispered.

She smiled.

Margrite and I walked out of the CPS building, hopefully for the last time. It sucked that I'd left a part of myself there.

But we had to go. If Nala and Marion were hearing things that meant the talk was pretty hot.

"She was worried," Margrite said.

"You noticed that too?"

"Yeah."

"It's good we're leaving."

"Yeah," I said.

By unspoken agreement, we headed back to the motel. It felt like we needed to get out of the open, needed to get to somewhere we'd be safe, have a door between us and the world.

We both went to bed early. Tomorrow was the day.

For a lot of reasons.

J woke with the sun. Quietly, I got dressed and went out to grab coffee and muffins. When I got back, Margrite was up.

"Thank God," she said. "I can't wait to have our place where we can keep coffee."

I nodded, and handed the coffee and muffin to her. We ate quickly, and she went and got ready. Stefan had said this morning. We had to leave by lunch. This show needed to get on the road.

The coffee was gone and both of us were feeling our nerves when the knock on the door came. I think we both jumped a foot off the beds.

"I got it," I said. I looked out the peephole. It was Stefan. Cautiously, I opened the door.

"Are you alone?"

He nodded. "My affairs are in order, and it's only me. I do have a car a distance from here, should things not go as planned."

I opened the door wider, and let him in. It was interesting to see him on his own. There was a difference. He wasn't the same man who walked in here yesterday.

"What are you worried about?" I didn't like the idea that he had his guys hanging around.

"That things may not go as I hoped. I'll need a ride home, in that case."

"Is Caleb with them?"

"He is."

Margrite made a noise that sounded like a snort.

"You should fire him. He can't find his way out of a paper bag."

Stefan shrugged. "He does what is needed. What now?" Stefan asked.

Margrite sat on the bed closest to the door. She didn't speak.

"You need to swear a blood bond now, to me, in front of

us," I said. I wasn't sure what I wanted him to swear, but I wanted to see how he reacted.

"A blood bond?" Stefan's eyebrows went up.

He was surprised though. It was faint, but I could see it. Good. I felt like it was better to keep this guy a little off balance.

"Yes."

"What is it exactly that you want me to swear to?"

"That you are telling me the truth, and that you have no hidden agenda. That you will not harm anyone who agrees to help you either returning to the Realm, or while you're in the Realms." The words came out in a rush. I didn't have any idea where they came from, but as I spoke them, I knew it was the right thing to say.

He eyed me. I gave him eyeball for eyeball. The silence stretched out, neither of us willing to give anything.

Then he looked down and sighed. "Very well."

What the hell do I do to get him to swear with all the right things, Fangorn? I yelled in my head.

Have him take your hand, and keep eye contact, and speak the words.

Okay, this wasn't weird at all. But like most things I found with the Dragon Realm, it was old-fashioned and formal and serious. I moved closer to Stefan and held out my hand.

He took it and met my eyes. "I swear, with my bond in my blood, that I am speaking the truth. I have no hidden agenda. I want to return to the Fae Realm to live the rest of my life, hopefully in peace. I will not harm anyone who helps me return, or helps me once I have returned to the Fae Realm. I will fulfill my promise to help find my brother, Eilor."

I felt my hand tighten around his, and something, I have no idea what, passed through me. Just like Fangorn said.

I am coming to you, Fangorn said.

What? I looked around. I had no idea where he'd make a portal. This wasn't a big room, and with three people, it was already cramped.

I don't think— I got out.

A light flashed, and Fangorn stepped through a portal.

Stefan jumped back.

Fangorn strode forward, no mean feat in this room, looming over Stefan. "You tell us where to find him, and if we do, I'll make it possible for you to return to the Fae Realm permanently."

Stefan just stared, then he said, "You wish for me to wait?" He shook his head. "I don't think so."

Fangorn crossed his arms. "This is your only chance. We will find him. And we will kill him. It may take longer, but I've waited over one thousand years. You have the choice to be part of that, or not."

Stefan didn't answer.

Fangorn stared back, and then turned away.

Stefan, moving so fast I didn't see it, grabbed Margrite and was back at the door, Margrite in front of him. He held a knife in his hand, and it was at her throat.

I was getting really tired of these assholes always trying to use my best friend. Margrite looked pissed. My dragon wanted to come out and take care of business. I tamped him down. For the moment, anyway.

"You will take me home, or I will end her."

Fangorn had turned when Stefan grabbed Margrite, and he didn't respond right away. Finally, he said, "Let go of her. You don't, and I will kill you."

I had to admire how calm he sounded.

Stefan, equally calm, said, "You and what army?"

Shift now, Fangorn said.

My dragon was practically banging down the door to shift, so it wasn't hard. As we shifted, I saw a line of flame erupt next to me. Fangorn shot flame next to Stefan's head, making him jump.

"What the hell, dragon?" Stefan yelled. He shoved Margrite from him. "All right, all right! Stop! Take her!"

Margrite stumbled and I caught her. She looked up as she

fell into the dragon me. "I'm okay."

"Doesn't mean we won't kill him," I said. It wasn't as quiet as I'd hoped.

Both Fangorn and Stefan focused on me.

"What? I was willing to give you a chance!" I said. "You swore an oath!"

"I didn't hurt her," Stefan said. "Nor did I plan to."

"Then why did you do it?" I glared, wanting to echo Fangorn and fry him.

Stefan looked ashamed. "Habit, I think."

"Thanks," Margrite rubbed her throat as she turned around. "Putting a knife on me was *habit*?" She took two steps and slapped Stefan.

The sound echoed in the room.

"He would be dead had he intended harm," Fangorn said. *Be calm, Aodan.*

I moved Margrite behind me as I got so close to Stefan he had no room to move and leaned against the door. "You do that again, and I won't give a damn about whatever oath you're trying to sidestep. I will *end* you." My dragon voice ended on a growl, and I was gratified to see that Stefan flinched a bit.

Fangorn placed a claw on my leg. "Aodan, I will handle this."

I didn't move, still glaring at Stefan. Then I huffed, smoke blowing out of my nostrils, and stepped back.

Turning his gaze back to Stefan, Fangorn said, "You've been gone for a long time. Perhaps too long. How can you be sure you'll have any information of value to offer?"

He has someone in the Realms who gives him info, or updates, or whatever.

Fangorn stilled. *Why didn't you tell me this before?*

I didn't have time.

Stefan said, not sounding at all like someone who had nearly had his head burned off, "Do not make assumptions about things you don't understand."

Fangorn huffed, and then said, "I'm going to take you back now. And you can tell the Dragon King your story."

You sure that's a good idea? I thought.

It's better to keep an eye on him. Come with me.

No. I need to get Margrite out of here. This is the second time she's been taken to hold over our heads. This shit is getting ridiculous.

It is ridiculous. Effective, but ridiculous. Get her out of here and join me in the Dragon Realm, he responded.

Out loud Fangorn said, "You have sworn your blood bond. I shall take you back with me. You will then need to prove yourself useful."

An expression I couldn't read crossed Stefan's face. He looked younger. "You do mean to bring me home?"

"You must answer for your past," Fangorn's tone was neutral.

"I will. I am tired of this Realm. Whatever it is I have done, and it is not all that you think, I have paid. This Realm has been my punishment."

"Hey," I began.

Stefan cut me off. "Once you live in the Realm, you will not wish to live elsewhere. I accept your agreement. You will speak for me with the king? Or whomever it is I must deal with?"

Fangorn nodded. "I will. But you will not set one foot out of line, or I shall end you myself. Is that clear?"

Stefan's face paled.

I thought, *Hey, you should know. I think he, and definitely Eilor, saw a person burned alive by a dragon*

I saw the slight change in Fangorn's expression, even in his dragon form.

That is one of the ways the fae used to utilize our power.

I tried not to frown. I didn't want Stefan to know we were talking. *The fae don't always sound so great.*

Fangorn shrugged. *The current king is a vast improvement. I didn't use to think so, but knowledge of the king and his sons has shifted my opinion.*

He spoke to Stefan again. "What do you need to do? We must leave."

Stefan nodded. "I'm ready."

I held up a claw. "I have a condition before Fangorn takes you."

Both Fangorn and Stefan looked at me. They were surprised, and I knew that Fangorn, at least, wasn't a fan of surprises.

"I want you to fire Caleb."

Stefan's brow lowered. "Why?"

"Because he doesn't deserve whatever you're leaving him in charge of."

"Why do you care?"

My voice hardened. "Because I've seen how he uses power."

Stefan's brow cleared, and he nodded. "That I understand."

"Call him. In front of us," I added. I'd been willing to trust him before he grabbed Margrite, but now … he had to prove himself each and every time.

Stefan pulled a phone from his pocket and spoke quietly into it.

I want to roar at him.

Who? Fangorn asked. *Stefan? You already have.*

No, his guy that he's calling.

Why do you hate this human man so much?

I shot a glance at Fangorn. *He tried to have me killed more than once. I just want to see him pee his pants.*

Fangorn sighed. *It's not very noble but … I suppose I can help.*

I don't care whether it's noble. He deserves it. More than this, probably.

There was a knock at the door.

"Answer it. If there is a danger to any of us, you and your man will die," Fangorn said.

Stefan turned and carefully opened the door. Caleb came in. "Boss, what's up?" He looked around.

And then, in the most beautiful thing I'd seen in a long time, he saw Fangorn, and me. He fell back against the door frame, his mouth opening and closing. His face got red, and I could tell that he was having a hard time breathing.

Beautiful.

Stefan crossed his arms. "Caleb, you continue to be useless. I have no need of your services any longer. Get out. I don't want to see you again. If I do, if I even hear of you, I will kill you."

Caleb's eyes widened, and his mouth worked harder, but no sounds came out. Finally, he said, "Boss."

"Go. Now. Before I lose patience."

What a psycho. No emotion at all. No wonder everyone and their brother was afraid of this guy.

Caleb stammered, "What? You can't—"

Stefan stood up straighter, and I could swear the guy grew a foot. "I can. And I am. And you will disappear. For good. If you want to keep living, you won't come back here."

Fangorn said quietly, "Now would be a good time to leave."

Caleb really was stupid. He blinked, and then looked from Stefan to Fangorn, not moving.

Now, Aodan, Fangorn thought.

We roared together.

Caleb's hands scrabbled for the door frame and he fell right onto his ass. He didn't even get up, but crab walked backward.

Stefan watched him for a moment, then shut the door behind him. He turned to look at the three of us. "Is that to your satisfaction?"

Margrite burst out laughing.

Fangorn said, "That is satisfactory."

I nodded.

Stefan said, "All right, then. I need ten minutes, and I'll be ready. This was not exactly what I planned for."

"I thought you didn't want to come back," I said.

"I plan even for eventualities I don't want," Stefan said.

"Do not try anything. You will die," Fangorn said, like he was ordering a coffee.

"I want to get home. I will do nothing to jeopardize that."

Fangorn reached out, claws extended and grabbed Stefan's hand. "You have sworn the bond of blood. It will not forget."

Stefan paled a little, and quickly left when Fangorn let go of him. The door shut behind him.

Fangorn looked between both of us. "Do you have the necklace that Eilor wore?"

Margrite shot a look at me. I nodded. I wondered how he'd figured it out. Probably not the time to ask.

Fangorn saw us. "Why did you not tell me?"

"I wasn't ready to. Plus, we didn't really talk about it."

Fangorn's eyes narrowed. His nostrils flared. "You knew— you both knew--what it meant to me. I told you how this was obtained."

I started to speak, and he held up a claw. I could feel the rising tension from him. It was like electricity let loose in the room. He was managing his anger.

He said, "I am furious. But I cannot speak of it at this moment. I will take the necklace now." He held out a claw.

Margrite reached around the back of her neck and pulled up the thick gold chain. The pendant came out from under her shirt, and after she took it off, she put it into Fangorn's outstretched claw.

He looked at her. "You were not afraid to have this next to your skin?"

"It's yours, isn't it?"

"I rather think that it was more Eilor's," Fangorn said.

Margrite shook her head. "No, that makes it just ugly and tacky. The thing that made it special—that was yours. Your blood, right?"

Fangorn answered her slowly. "Yes."

She shrugged. "You're part of Aodan's family. He's my family. Family doesn't screw family."

"What do you call lying to me about this?" He split his glare between the two of us.

"Selective sharing of facts. We wouldn't have kept it," she

shot back.

I ducked my head down so that the grin wouldn't be as obvious. It was rare I saw anyone match Margrite. She was too smart, too quick. Even with Fangorn.

When I felt it was safe for me to look up, I saw they were glaring at one another. Neither was willing to give an inch.

Fangorn sighed. "You're telling the truth."

Margrite said, "Hey- no brain scans or any funny stuff! Keep that for yourselves!"

Fangorn said, rather dryly, "Refresh my memory. Did not the funny stuff allow us come to you?"

She crossed her arms. "Another reason to get the hell out of here. If we're not always on the verge of dying, no funny stuff would be necessary."

"We are leaving," I said.

Her eyes brightened. "Really? Finally?"

Fangorn said, "Yes."

"Thank God," she breathed. She turned away from the door where we all still stood, pushing past me.

I looked at my grandfather. *I am sorry.*

He sighed. *I cannot forgive at this moment.*

I understand.

But I will. I need time.

Okay. What else could I say?

A knock on the door brought us back to the business at hand. I opened it. Stefan slid in, shutting it behind him quickly.

"I'm ready."

Fangorn glared at him. "Remember your oath."

Stefan nodded. "I will."

Shift back, but be ready, Fangorn thought.

We both shifted, and I immediately went into a crouch, ready to spring at Stefan if I had to.

He'd flattened himself up against the door. "I've never seen that before," he said.

Fangorn said briskly, "Don't concern yourself with our

affairs." Reaching into a pocket, he pulled out a stone, and opened a portal before I could barely blink. "Let's go."

Stefan didn't move.

"He means you," I said.

Stefan blinked, and then he stepped closer to the portal. He looked back.

"Go," Fangorn said.

Stefan stepped in, slowly. Almost as if he wasn't sure he wanted to go now.

Maybe it was a case of being careful of what you wished for. I didn't know. Right now, I didn't care. I needed them out of our room.

Fangorn stepped in after Stefan.

Be safe, I thought.

He turned around. *You as well. Get her safe, and then contact me. Do not delay.*

I will. I promise.

Stop hiding things from me.

I frowned. *Stop glaring. And you need to listen to your own advice. You've got your own hiding to worry about. Probably things I should know. I'm not a kid.*

He rolled his eyes. *Yes, you are. Now go.* "Good bye, Margrite. Safe travels."

"Bye," she said. She almost sounded wistful.

What was that all about? The portal closed, and Margrite turned to me.

"Can we please get out of here? Before someone or something else tries to stop us?"

"Absolutely. Let's finish the packing, and get to the airport."

We were both good at bugging out quickly, but I think this was our fastest one ever. With Caleb on the loose, and the talk both Nala and Marion had told us about, we needed to be gone like yesterday.

I smiled as we roared past the sign proclaiming the city limits.

12

*I*t was time to get in touch. *Fangorn?*

He took a moment to reply. *Things are interesting.*

How so?

Stefan is … interesting.

Is he actually helping, or going through the motions, or being a pain in the ass?

He is trying to help, as far as I can tell. He is also sincere, as far as I can tell. We have not, of course, found Eilor.

I thought he knew all the hiding places. I'd wondered if Stefan had stretched his knowledge.

Fangorn said, *He does know some good ones. I know the Realm well, and there were two I was unaware of. The rest he showed us were not places I would think fae knew of.*

Well, then hopefully that burns some of Eilor's safe houses.

Precisely. Two showed signs of someone being there recently. There is no way to tell if that someone was Eilor.

So I take it Stefan's met all the people he needs to? Is he getting to stay?

I think so. Under careful watch. Aine lets him know his every move is tracked. Amusement came through on that one.

I laughed.

Are you and Margrite safe?

I think so. We took five flights under five different names to get here. Name number five bought this. It's in her name, not mine. She has enough to live, with or without me.

I didn't want to admit it, but I was afraid I wouldn't be able to enjoy our new life. And I wanted to be sure that Margrite would be safe, or at least be able to buy her way to safety. I'd put everything in her name. She didn't know that. At least, not yet.

I will come to you tomorrow. I think I have a way to make sure Margrite stays safe. I have been thinking of your words--that people use her to get to you, and through you to me. I need to make sure she is safe. Otherwise she will always be used as a threat.

Well that makes me want to jump right on whatever bandwagon you've got.

We need you here, Aodan. There are things we need your help with. That cannot happen if Margrite is constantly used against you.

That's one thing we agree on.

I know that's not what you want to hear.

I shook my head even though he couldn't see me. *I'll talk to you when you get here.*

Fangorn said, *Aodan--*

I shut the door between us.

What was going on? Once again, big dragon schemes, although at least he's added in looking out for M. At least it's not just me.

One thing I'd learned since this whole dragon thing started. Nothing would change whatever was headed my way, and I should probably eat. Fangorn showed up and things like regular meals kind of fell by the wayside.

Which was weird. I'd always thought of dragons as roaming around eating some poor farmer's sheep, or something like that.

I didn't say anything to Margrite. She was in the kitchen, humming as she cut up fruit and fixed dinner. The job I'd done made this possible. All that we had done, all that we had suffered, had made this possible.

I hoped it would last.

I also couldn't remember the last time I'd heard her hum.

"Come and eat," she said.

I ate. And then went to bed. Whatever was going to happen was going to happen.

That night, if I dreamed, I didn't remember it, and I didn't wake up.

When I woke the next morning, the sun shone cheerfully into my bedroom window. I sighed and stretched, taking my time. I'd have to tell Margrite about Fangorn. She'd be mad if he showed up and I hadn't warned her.

No time like the present, right? I got dressed and went into the living room. She was already up, and in the kitchen again.

"What is it with you and the kitchen?"

She looked up at me, and then rolled her eyes. "You're such a Neanderthal. Look at this kitchen! It's gorgeous. Everything here is new, and it all works. Neither of us has to worry about electrocuting ourselves, or getting botulism from spoiled food."

"It was not that bad," I protested.

"It was bad enough. But this is beautiful, and it's ours. It makes me want to be in here."

"Well, good. Make me some eggs," I said.

She threw a dishtowel at me.

Laughing, I went and sat out on the front porch. The cottage looked out over the ocean. I hadn't seen the ocean before we came to the islands, and it was honestly one of the most gorgeous things I'd ever seen. What I liked was that it went on and on. I mean, I know it doesn't go on forever, but there's something appealing about looking out in front of you and seeing nothing but the wide open.

There are a lot of possibilities in that.

I haven't even had coffee yet, I groused. *Much less breakfast.*

Well, get some of it, and I will be with you shortly.

He sounded grim. Great. I headed back in, my peace done for the time being. Probably for quite some time.

"Got any coffee?"

"Of course. And it's good."

"Good. We need it."

"Why?" Her entire bearing changed, becoming still and watchful.

"Fangorn's on his way."

She didn't say anything but let out a huge sigh. "Just when I thought we'd get a break."

"Apparently not."

"Does he like coffee and breakfast?"

"I don't know."

She frowned. "I'll make extra. When's he coming?"

"Um … now."

"Thanks for the warning, A!"

I shrugged. "You get a little less than me, but not much less."

"Go away," she grumbled.

A few minutes later, after I'd made a cup of coffee, a light popped into being in our living room. It grew large enough to allow a man to pass through, and then Fangorn was in front of us.

He came to me and embraced me. Then he turned to Margrite, who'd come over to stand next me. He put his hands on her shoulders. "You are well?"

"Yes."

"The time in the Realm didn't harm you? I did not have a chance to ask you before. If something had gone awry, you would have noticed it by now."

She shrugged. "I don't know. I faked being sick, so I looked worse than I was. I didn't feel great, but I wasn't as bad as I looked."

"That is interesting. We should—"

She held up hand. "No. We shouldn't do a thing. I like where I am. Aodan and I have worked hard for this, and this is where I am going to stay." She smiled, and it was unexpected. It lit up her entire face.

I could see that it surprised Fangorn as well.

"I'm turning over a new leaf, and since I am, I'll offer you some eggs and coffee."

Fangorn nodded. "I accept," he said.

"Then come in and sit down. Let's eat before you dump the bad news on us."

He looked like he was about to protest, and I stopped him. "Twenty minutes isn't going to make or break things, is it?"

"No."

"Then sit."

"Yeah, before I throw you your eggs," Margrite added.

Fangorn was not slow on the uptake. He talked with Margrite about how she was feeling, and he was interested in how we'd made it here. He was trying.

"So you will live under different names?"

"Yes. Neither of us want to have anyone from back there looking for us."

He nodded, taking a large bite of fruit. "That is wise. It's not a bad thing to hide from one's enemy."

"What if you can't?" Margrite asked, her words challenging.

Fangorn smiled then, and the picture he presented was so chilling it made all the hairs on my body stand up. "You kill them."

"Great," I stared down at my plate. Killing anyone wasn't on my agenda, outside of Eilor.

Fangorn shrugged. "I don't want to die. Not yet. There's more to be done. I don't want you to die, nor, I am sure, do you wish to die now, just as you've gotten all that you were seeking."

"No, I don't," I said.

It wasn't all. I knew what else was missing. But I wasn't going to say it.

You don't have to.

I heard the voice in my head.

I don't want to upset everything here.

You belong somewhere else, Aodan.

I looked at him, but his expression was bland as he chewed a piece of toast.

That's not fair. Not to me, not to Margrite.

Fangorn blinked slowly, then turned his gaze onto her.

"Margrite, may we speak of your time in the Dragon Realm?"

"What do you want to know?" She didn't look up from her plate.

That wasn't a good sign.

"What did he do to you?" Fangorn asked in one of the most gentle tones I'd ever heard from him.

I saw her shoulders flinch, and then she took a deep breath and raised her head.

The pain in her eyes made a cut through my heart. It had been worse than she'd let on.

13

"He didn't touch me," Margrite hastened to say, directing her words to me. "I didn't lie to you. He didn't lay a finger on me. He didn't have to," her voice ended in a whisper.

"What did he do?" I ground out.

"I told you," she got up and wrapping her arms around herself, went to the window, leaving us staring at her back. "He likes to talk. He's in love with the sound of his own voice. You know the type," she glanced at me briefly over her shoulder.

I could see the look on her face, and I smiled. "Yeah," I said.

"He told me what a waste of your time I was," her head swiveled back to the window. "He made sure I knew all the things that were there for you over there—over in the Dragon Realm. He told me I was keeping you from greatness. From..." her voice dropped. "From the throne."

"He said that?" Fangorn got up, moving closer to Margrite.

She didn't look around again, only hugged herself tighter, her head nodding. "Yes."

Fangorn stopped next to her. He put his hands on her shoulders. "There is nothing that you are keeping Aodan from. He is a child of two worlds, of three peoples. He must walk a line to find his own place, because all three of his places call to him."

"Am I holding him back?" Her voice was soft, not like I was used to hearing from her.

"No." Fangorn's voice was definite. "Aodan is not in line for any throne, no matter whether he wants it or not," he glanced over at me and smiled briefly.

"I don't," I said.

"I know that," Fangorn said, not looking at me. "So does Margrite."

"He sounded so sure."

I didn't like this tone, this manner from her. It made me uneasy. I joined them at the window, putting my arm around her shoulder.

"He's not sure of anything, other than he's an asshole," I said. "And there is nothing that Eilor has that I want, nothing he's involved in that has any interest to me. I mean, other than wiping the floor with him when I get the chance." I leaned down so she could see me. "You can't trust anything he says."

"It's difficult," Fangorn crossed his arms, gazing out at the water in front our cottage. "Eilor is skilled at exposing and exploiting the doubts of others."

"You're doubting me?" I asked.

"You know I have been." Margrite didn't shy away from it.

"I'm where I want to be," I said. I felt Fangorn look toward me, and I didn't move my head, or acknowledge him in any way.

"Well, things change," Margrite said. "So you know it. He didn't touch me, didn't hurt me, but he talked to me, about his plans, about the things I was keeping you from—he talked until I was ready to off myself just to have a little quiet."

"What did he say he was planning to do?" Fangorn asked.

"Did he get any of your blood?" Margrite asked me.

"No. He started to take it, but that's about the time the rest of the dragons busted in."

"I would have liked to have seen that."

"You'll meet them," I said.

"Is that even allowed?" Margrite directed this to Fangorn.

"Usually, no, it is not. But for our family, our loved ones, we allow it." He smiled.

A feeling of warmth flowed through me.

Thank you.

You're welcome. I like Margrite, I like her very much. But I am not sure your paths are meant to stay together.

Did you see the memory I shared with Aine?

Yes.

It was my parents.

He didn't respond immediately. *I know,* he finally said.

"Hey! Are you guys mind melding?" Margrite glared at both of us.

"Yes. I am sorry, I slip into it with my brethren," Fangorn said.

"What are you saying?"

"I was telling him that I saw my parents and shared it with Aine. And I was thanking him for inviting you into the Dragon Realm," I said.

I wouldn't lie to her.

"But we cannot know if it makes you ill," Fangorn said.

"What?" I asked.

Margrite walked away, out onto the porch. I could see her, hands on hips, gazing out at the ocean. As far as stress relievers went, it was a pretty good one.

"Did I say something wrong?" Fangorn asked me in a low tone.

"Not that I'm aware of. She'll be back."

He smiled, and we both waited. When she came in, her face had the look of someone who had made a decision.

"Okay. I'm ready. Lay it on me."

"Lay what on you?" Fangorn looked confused.

"I don't know you well, but I can totally see when you're

hatching some kind of plan, and hoping like mad it works. Aodan is the same way. I just needed to adjust my mental state to that kind of thing again."

Fangorn stared at her, and then burst out laughing. I don't think I'd ever seen him like this, and it made me feel good—no, great—that he was letting Margrite into the other part of my life. His being unguarded was a good sign. I hoped she recognized that.

"What I was saying, before you walked away, was that I would welcome you to the Dragon Realm, but we cannot know if it makes you ill. I did not observe you while you were there, and I am unsure if Eilor enhanced your weakness in any manner. However, I think I have a solution."

From his pouch, he drew out Eilor's necklace. "How did you come by this, if you do not mind me asking?" He set the necklace on the table between them.

Margrite smiled. "I stole it from asshat when he dumped me through the portal. He was all atwitter over having Aodan, so he didn't even notice."

"I'm sure he's noticed now," Fangorn said.

"Maybe, but maybe not with the reasons you're thinking," I said.

"What do you mean?"

I walked back to the table, sitting down and taking up my coffee cup. "Right as he was about to take blood from me, you guys burst in. I don't know all the details, but he must have hauled ass out of there. He wasn't thinking of anything other than staying alive. And you guys destroyed the place, right?"

Fangorn nodded.

"Then he might assume he lost it in the fight, or whatever. And if you destroyed his little hideout, then he might think the pendant is destroyed also."

Fangorn sat down to the side of me. "That's possible."

"I think you need to assume that he knows everything,"

Margrite came over and topped off our cups with coffee. "He's usually ahead of you."

"Well, we have Stefan now," I smiled. "How's he working out?"

Fangorn rolled his eyes. "He is … a trial at times. I don't know how Drake hasn't just put a sword through him and been done with it. Like Eilor, Stefan likes to hear himself talk—"

"Oh, what a lovely family trait," I said.

"Both Drake and Brennan are diligently working through the places Stefan is taking him."

"Do you trust him?" Margrite sat down.

"No, I do not. I cannot," He added. "But I shall use him if he continues to be useful. Once he is no longer useful, he will have a choice."

"Of what?" She asked.

"Of whether he wishes to live out his life in quiet in one of the Realms, or if I kill him."

"Does he know that?" That wasn't the agreement we made with him. I didn't want this coming back to bite any of us. It's not like we didn't have a strong enough enemy. If Stefan teamed up with his brother because he was mad at the current kings—

"Of course he does. He is a man of the Realms. He understands. I think that he's been in the Human Realm long enough that his desire to be home is stronger than his familial ties."

"He hates Eilor," I said. "Eilor set him up."

"We have only Stefan's word. It's true that he took all the blame, but there is no surety in his words."

"Great family," Margrite said.

"Not all the nobles are truly noble."

"No shit," I said.

"The fae and the dragons do not do everything the same. Because we can all see into the hearts of one another, we cannot lie to each other."

"Yeah, tell me about it."

"It's hard when you haven't been accustomed to it,"

Fangorn said. "But you will become more comfortable. Aine didn't grow up with it, but she's adapted well."

"Even when she wants to keep fae business from you?" I asked.

"There's always room for privacy. But we do not lie. We can withhold, for our sake, or the sake of courtesy. There's no room for lies." He turned to Margrite. "I thank you for stealing this, but now, I wish you to have it."

She shrugged. "I figured he'd had it long enough. But why do you want me to have it?"

"You could have kept it."

"You wouldn't have known?"

Fangorn smiled. "We would have."

Margrite shrugged again. "I know. I'm well aware. Besides, I hated that he had something he stole from you and then used against you."

"Correct me if I'm wrong, but didn't the two of you steal?" His eyebrows went up.

"We stole to live. We didn't use the things we stole, and we didn't work with assholes."

"Well, Luke is kind of borderline," Margrite said.

"Whatever your reasons, or your ethics, I am pleased you returned this to me. I am in your debt, Margrite." He inclined his head regally.

Margrite blushed. I couldn't remember the last time I'd seen her do that. Great. Gramps was winning over my best friend.

"You don't owe me anything."

"But I do. I've wanted this back for a long time. You have aided me personally. Additionally, you have removed a weapon from the hands of Eilor. Now he is without the ring of the Dragon Realm, and his necklace. He'll have to do things making guesses. He will make a mistake."

"Don't underestimate him," Margrite said.

"I don't think anyone does," I said.

"I know better than most what he is capable of," Fangorn said. A shadow crossed his face, and it didn't leave.

"You want to see what I saw more directly?" I moved back to the subject of my memory with my parents.

His head turned to me so quickly I was sure he'd hurt himself.

"From your parents? Yes. Do you have some of their things?"

"I do. Why don't you come with me, and I'll show you?" We both got up.

As we headed toward my room, Margrite called out, "Hey, don't mind me! I cooked, so I'll be just delighted to clean it up, too!"

"I'll get the dishes," I said, loud enough that she could hear.

"Yeah, you will. I'm going to the beach."

I stopped and turned around. "What? Since when are you a beach person?"

"Since we live across from one. Go," she made a shooing motion with her hands. "It's nice to not be worrying about whatever the fate of the world is. I'll be back later."

I watched as she got a bag from her room, slipped on her flip flops, pulled a hat from the bag, and walked out the door.

"I don't even know her anymore," I muttered.

"Or perhaps you just don't know her now. She seems far more carefree than she's ever been."

"It's this place. It's relaxing, and freeing."

"But you are neither," he eyed me. "Are you?"

I let out a sigh, tossing myself into a chair in my room. "No. I'm not sleeping. I keep seeing Eilor, and Margrite, and I dream about flying and trying to grab things just out of reach."

"You are meant to be where you can let your dragon self out."

"I'm not part of your world!"

"You are, and always will be. You don't have to be there, but you will dream of flying for the rest of your life."

I stared, and he didn't say anything else for a couple of minutes.

"Let me see what you got from your parents. How did you come to get these things?"

That was an effective change of subject. Blunt, no pretense. Today, I'd take it. I got up and brought out the box from Marion.

Fangorn sifted through it, coming across the box that held the ring. He opened it and when he saw it was empty, he waved it at me.

"I'm wearing it," I said, holding up a hand.

"May I?"

I slid it off, not really wanting to give it to him. My hand felt naked without it.

He turned it over in his hands, his lips moving. But whatever he was saying was not out loud. Finally, he looked up at me, his fingers still cradling the ring. "This is extraordinary."

14

"What do you mean?" I said.

"I can feel him in here," Fangorn said softly.

It didn't feel like he was talking to me.

The door creaked, and I saw that Margrite had come back in. "I forgot water," she said. She was watching Fangorn with a look on her face that could only be described as pity. "You miss him."

Fangorn looked up quickly. "I do. Every day. I miss all my children. The ones I watched grow whom I lost in the war. The ones who only took a few breaths and then moved on. I remember them all," his voice growled on the last word. "Until you, Aodan, and Aine, Lionel was my last child. He was taken from me in such a manner that I gave up hope. When I realized that Aine was still alive. I allowed myself to hope. Then I discovered you, and my hope doubled." He closed his eyes. "But even having more hope now than I thought possible, it doesn't reduce missing the others."

"I'm sorry," I said, unsure of what to say.

"There is nothing for you to be sorry for. You have done

none of this, and you are behaving admirably. But now that breakfast is done, may we speak of what brought me here?"

"You don't want to see more of what is in the box?"

"I do, but I can tell that if I allow myself to venture too far into memory, I will not stay focused on my mission at hand. We must never forget those who are gone, but it is more important to do for the living first," he said, giving me a rare smile. "The box will still be here when my concern has been addressed. And you have allowed me a part of my son that I didn't have before. Thank you." He handed the ring back to me.

I slid it back on my finger. It felt right, like it should be there.

To me, when Fangorn smiled, I could see what it looked like just before he ate something. The ferocity in his grin wasn't disguised by his pleasure.

That is life as a dragon, he thought.

To always look like you're about to eat something?

To take immense pleasure in where you are at the moment. We know this more than most.

"Stop it," Margrite said. "No head talk. I can hear what you're saying without collapsing in a heap."

"You can. Aodan was merely thinking I looked like I was about to eat something."

"You do," she said.

"Well, that's good. It keeps those around me guessing."

"Even us?" Margrite lifted a brow.

Was she flirting with him? What the hell?

Fangorn laughed, recognizing her teasing.

"I like both of you very much, so I do not think I shall be eating you anytime soon."

Aodan?

I heard Aine.

What?

What is Fangorn doing?

Laughing, he answered her.

Silence, then, *Oh.*

Fangorn laughed again. "Apparently I need to laugh more. My other daughter just expressed concern for me. If you'll excuse me?" He directed this at Margrite.

She nodded.

His other daughter? Was there another one we didn't know about? I felt like I could barely keep up with this conversation, like everyone was talking around me, and I was wrapped in something that kept me from hearing everything.

I didn't like it.

I am fine, he said. *I am laughing with Aodan and Margrite. I realized I have the young around me once more, and they cannot be taken away. It made me happy. I am sorry to alarm you.*

I'm glad you're happy, Aine thought.

You are the entire reason I've come to this point, Fangorn thought.

He'd gotten to her concern a lot quicker than I had.

Aine was jealous.

No sooner than I'd thought it, her response came back. *I am. It's not very noble, but I am.*

Dragons guard what is ours fiercely, Fangorn thought. *But with each other, we can learn to share. In that vein, I am going to give Margrite the pendant she stole from Eilor.*

What? She took it from him?

I'd forgotten Aine probably wouldn't know this.

"You are?" I asked.

"What?" Margrite said.

I held up a hand. "Hang on. Almost done, promise."

She did. She stole it as he sent her back to the Human Realm, and she gave it to back to me before I brought Stefan back. I've been so concerned with him, I forgot to share this with all of you. But I must bring Aodan back to us, and I want her to be able to call for help should she need it.

That is unexpected, I thought.

It is, he admitted. *I did not expect to want another to have it, but I like Margrite, and she will not have you to alert us should anyone find her here.*

I'm glad you care about her.

You love her. How can we not? This from Aine.

As I love you, Fangorn sent to Aine.

I know, Grandfather. My dragon apparently does not feel like sharing.

That will pass.

I hope you are right, she thought. *I do not care for the smallness of this feeling.*

We will see you soon, Daughter, Fangorn thought.

Let me know when you are back in the Dragon Realm.

I felt her leave, as though she'd shut a door. This must be what it felt like.

"Well?" Margrite looked impatient.

"Her dragon? Did she shift?" I asked Fangorn.

"Not yet, but I think it's coming."

"How does that work? Aodan didn't have to think about it at all."

"I do not know. I suppose it is different for each fae dragon shifter. I would like to blame Eilor for some of it, just because I feel he deserves all the blame that can be laid at his doorstep."

"You meant it about the pendant?" I asked.

"What about it?" Margrite searched our faces.

"I want you to keep it," he picked it up from the table and handed it to her, closing his hands around hers. "I will need to bring Aodan to the Dragon Realm, and I want you to have a way to contact him, contact us. I have been thinking about how those who wish to influence Aodan attempt to go through you."

"Yeah, it's a little tiring," she said.

"This way, you can communicate with all of us. Put it on."

Slowly, Margrite slipped the necklace over her head. As the pendant settled down to her chest, she gasped.

"Holy shit!"

"You feel us." Fangorn's voice left no room for questions.

"My God, I do. Is this what it's like?" She looked at me. "Why didn't I feel this before?"

"Because we did not know you had it, and you were hiding

it. That would be my guess," Fangorn answered her last question.

"You need to learn to shut the door," I said, answering her first.

"I don't understand what that means." She looked panicked.

"Take all the noise, whatever you see or hear or feel, and shove it behind a door. Then close it. Hard." I reached across and took her hand.

She squeezed it, and then abruptly let it go. "Oh, shit. I need you not to touch me. It makes things louder."

"Maybe she shouldn't have it," I said.

"No, I want this, but I have to figure out how to live with it. It's like it woke up, or something. Cut me some slack," she glared at me. "You've had a couple of weeks to get used to it."

Welcome, Margrite, Fangorn's voice said.

I felt the presence of the others.

Then a chorus of '*Welcome*' came through.

Is this acceptable to you, Fangorn?

It was a deeper tone, a male I didn't recognize.

Yes, Ynos, it is. Is this acceptable to all of you?

Yes. The word whispered through all of us.

Margrite looked like she was going to faint.

Are you all right? I thought.

Her head jerked toward me. *How did—* She stopped her own thought.

"I heard you," she breathed.

Duh.

Shut up, she thought.

If this is acceptable to Fangorn, I am in agreement, a new voice broke in.

It was Aine.

But you must keep this safe, Margrite, she continued. Eilor would love to have it back. And Fangorn, we need to—

I know, he cut her off.

What was that all about?

"I will," Margrite said. "Oh, shit."

I will, she said via thought.

I smiled at her.

"I don't know," she muttered. "This is so weird."

You can talk to any of us, I heard from Fangorn. *Any one of us will help you if you need it.*

Thank you, I heard from Margrite. *I … I'm honored that you would do this for me.*

There was silence after her thought. Then I felt approval. I felt my dragon brethren searching, looking into Margrite.

I wondered if she could feel it.

You are speaking truth, the deeper male voice said.

What had Fangorn called him? Ynos?

I'm trying. And I'm trying not to pee my pants, Margrite said. *You guys sound scary as shi—I mean, really big and scary.*

We are, Ynos said. *To those we don't like. But I think we shall like you fine.*

Feel better? I asked.

Not yet, she answered.

I could hear dragon chuckles.

Wise human, another voice said.

We are here if you need us, Fangorn said.

That seemed to end the conversation, and I felt the others fade.

"Is it like that for you all the time?"

"It was. Now I like it. Speaking of which, you were going to show me how to shut off the group think," I reminded Fangorn.

His brow wrinkled and then smoothed. "I did. It wasn't that long ago but it feels like quite some time ago."

"It does. But I could use something more solid, and I think Margrite could too."

"This is your door thing?" Margrite said to me.

I nodded.

"What was Aine talking about?" I asked.

"The reason you must come home with me."

"Which is?"

"Voko is ill."

In those three words, I felt all the weight of his worry, his concern. I thought about the older dragon, gold and gentle. Fangorn had told me she was like the mother of the group.

"What can I do?"

Fangorn sighed. "It's not a normal illness, whatever it is that is plaguing her."

"What is it?"

"We think—and she is the one who brought the idea forward—that she was poisoned."

"Who would do that?" I asked.

"Eilor. Who else?" Margrite asked.

"God, that guy is like an STD," I said.

"What is that?" Fangorn asked.

"Never mind. How did he get a poison to her that she actually took?"

"I don't know. I don't know that it's Eilor. For all I know, it's Stefan."

"You didn't bring him near the Caverns, did you?"

"Of course not. But he's been with me some of the time he was in the Realm, and he might have … I don't know what he might have done. I am going a little mad trying to puzzle this out. I cannot find where he might have had any opportunity to harm her. It not Stefan, then who? I can only guess it was Eilor. If he can reach her, and she does not leave the Caverns…"

"He can get to anyone," I said. "And he wants me, and my blood, and he wants in the Caverns. That's his goal."

"What does he think he's going to get there?" Margrite asked.

"The Caverns of the Ancients is where we bury our fallen. Those lost in the Dragon War are buried there. It's where we are the most powerful, because we can draw on the strength of our ancestors. It's where the other ten dragons reside. We feel safer there than anywhere else in all the Realms."

"You said only dragons could get in there … or maybe Eilor did. But you said we could have brought Margrite there." I was confused.

"It is only for dragons. Wearing that pendant, Eilor might have been able to make his way in. He was carrying part of me. This ring, which has some of Lionel's blood in it, could allow him access. Had we brought Margrite back, we would have warded her with our magic to make the Caverns safe for her."

"No wonder he wants in," Margrite went back to the table and sat down. "Should I wear this thing all the time?"

"Yes."

"It's not exactly island wear."

"You can wear it under things," I said. "Since when do you dress all beachy?"

"Since we moved to a beach." She glared.

"Have you heard from him?" I asked.

"No, and that concerns me. If it is not Eilor, what is it? Or whom? Very few even know we're there."

"So how can I help again?"

"Chevym—you have not met him yet—he is one of the strongest of us with magic. He will attempt to discover what has been done to her. We need the help of all the dragons. You and Aine must be there. We need the power of all of us."

"Isn't she the one who healed you?" Margrite asked.

I nodded. The thought of her sick made my chest ache.

"She is. She is the closest thing we have to a mother of the clan. But first, let us practice allowing you to shut a door within your mind."

He went through what we needed to do. It was like what I'd been doing, although when I practiced as he instructed, this felt easier, more streamlined. It took less effort for me.

By the end of his lesson however, Margrite was looking a little sweaty. "I think I've got it. I'll need to practice some more."

"You should. The easier it feels, the less you will need to

think about doing it, which can help if you find yourself in a less than ideal situation."

Margrite looked at him and started to laugh. "That's one way of putting it!"

"I will contact you after we leave, and we will practice together," Fangorn said to her. "In the meantime, when you hear us speaking, practice closing us off. We never will go away completely, but you can put up a barrier."

Thank you, she thought.

Are you worried?

I am always worried when I'm not with you. You tend to get stupid. But your grandpa isn't, so I have to assume you'll live in spite of yourself.

Thanks, I thought.

She smiled.

"May we go now?" Fangorn looked calm, but I could feel his impatience.

"Will you be all right?" I asked Margrite.

"I am better than I can ever remember. No one cares about me here. I'll have the house all to myself, and you're only a call away. Go. Help her." She gave me a slight shove with one hand.

This felt rushed, and I felt slightly handled, although whether by Margrite, or Fangorn, I wasn't sure.

"What do I need?"

"Nothing. We can portal right from here."

I leaned down and hugged Margrite. "Don't be stupid. Call if you need help. There's more than one of us."

She smiled, and I was struck again at how relaxed and content she looked, even as I could see worry on her features. We were right to come here. I was glad we'd done it. It just sucked that I had to leave before I could enjoy it.

Fangorn walked around the table and bent to kiss the top of her head. "We are not blood, but you are family, Margrite. You are the family of my grandson, and that makes you family. Please do not hesitate to call should you need assistance."

When he stood up, I could see her eyes shining. She was about to cry.

I understood now how Aine felt. All my anger at the things I didn't know, or his agenda, or whatever, fell away.

What the hell?

angorn didn't say anything else, only stepped into the middle of the room and waved his hand.

I noticed that he didn't need to use a stone all the time like the fae did.

Our magic is not theirs, he said.

How is it different? I asked as I watched the small light expand and stretch in front of me.

Ours comes from within. We all have the ability, although some are more skilled than others. We can also draw on the strength of other dragons. It's why we were so formidable.

Why did you lose?

Because all the fae and goblins and dwarves and trolls, combined with the Fae and Goblin Kings were more than we could handle. But only by a small amount, he added as he stepped through the portal.

I looked at Margrite and waved a hand. She waved back, smiling.

The smile seemed genuine.

I stepped into the portal, turning once more to see my friend. She was still smiling as the portal closed and the light went out.

We were back in the Caverns of the Ancients.

Even more than before, I felt like I was coming home. The weight of all the dragons here, of the dragons that had once lived here, wrapped around me like a blanket.

I'd taken three steps when I saw that I'd shifted.

Fangorn had shifted also, and he made a sound that could have been a laugh. *It's hard to resist the pull of our home.*

It is. Where is she?

Follow me.

The feeling in the cavern was different this time. Heavier, weightier. *What--?*

They know. They wish to help. They are here for whatever we may need.

I followed Fangorn, feeling more comfortable in my dragon skin than I had since the first time I'd shifted. We moved down a dark passage, passing several openings, but Fangorn didn't pause.

When he stopped, it was abrupt, and I nearly ran into him.

In here. He turned to the right, ducking his head to enter.

All the dragons were in here. The ones I'd met, and—I counted—the ones I hadn't. Aine stood near the green dragon I thought was Imi. Aine was leaning against her, her hands twisting in front of her.

She looked up as we entered.

She is still suffering, Aine said.

Has she worsened?

No, Imi said. *But neither is she better.*

We are all here.

Another green dragon moved forward to be closer to Voko, who lay on her side, breathing heavily.

Chevym, are you prepared?

Yes, the green male's voice was the same timber as Fangorn's. *I am glad to see you back. I began to worry.*

Aodan is a child of two Realms. He could not take his leave in haste.

That was a nice way to phrase it.

Welcome again, young one, Chevym inclined his head to me. *It is good to see you and Aine together. You are as you should be.*

What do we need to do to help her?

I couldn't help but stare at Voko. She looked so helpless. I hated it.

Gather round, brothers and sisters. We will ask our ancestors to help us as we search for what brings our mother low. Chevym lifted his head toward the ceiling.

I looked up and there was, high above us, an opening to the sky.

Chevym turned and the other dragons came into a circle. I moved closer, making sure to stand near Aine.

I'm glad you're here, she thought. Her hand slipped into my claw.

As am I, I thought. It was odd that being here brought out more formal speech than I'd ever used in my life. I wasn't sure I liked it. I did not want to sound like Fangorn, much as I liked him.

Next to me, I felt Aine make a sound that might have been a laugh.

Send forth your magic, and let me lean on you, Chevym thought.

The other dragons leaned their heads back, most closing their eyes. I couldn't look away—I'd never seen anything like this. The energy in this cavern was practically tangible.

A hum began, low, and just one or two dragons. Gradually, it grew until it reverberated around the cavern. It should have been deafening. It should have scared the pants off me.

But since I wasn't currently wearing them—they were absorbed in my shift somehow, for which I thanked all the deities that ever were—neither me or my pants were scared.

The hum grew louder, and I could hear Chevym saying something in a language I didn't understand. I didn't know the dragons had their own speech. Was it fae? Add that to the things I needed to ask Fangorn.

Voko stirred on the ground. Chevym kept speaking but he watched her carefully.

He held up his claws and the humming stopped.

The quiet was eerie.

I have it, he thought to the rest of us. *She is bound by the spell of another. It's a spell that keeps her from making any magic of her own, and instead, siphons off her energy, her strength.*

Gee, who could that be? The thought came out before I could stop it.

Chevym looked right at me. *I agree it's probably that midden heap Eilor, but we cannot know for sure.*

We must find him, an orange-red dragon thought.

Her voice was familiar.

The fae are searching for him as well, Ymri, and they have the brother of Eilor with them. Fangorn's voice broke in.

We could just question him ourselves, she thought, and her eyes glinted.

There it was. The dragon on the hunt.

I was a dragon, and she scared me.

Her head turned to me. *I told you I was the Taker of Life,* she thought, and her lips stretched into a dragon grin. *I shall enjoy the taking of Eilor's life.*

We will scatter him to the fires of this Realm, a tall orange dragon thought. *But we must find him first.*

Chevym, can you work with Gramuss and Imi to keep Voko comfortable? Fangorn looked around at the dragons.

Of course, the green male nodded.

Fangorn turned to Aine and I. *We must go to the fae kings and see if we might … encourage Stefan to greater motivation.*

Holy hell. Now his eyes were glinting, too. The sight made me feel strong and powerful.

A light blue dragon, cool and icy looking, moved closer. *You must hurry. We cannot allow her to fade.* She leaned forward, and a claw stroked Aine's cheek. *Then we can return to our lessons.*

Aine smiled briefly. *I am eager to do so, but I could not concentrate.*

The blue dragon nodded. *Nor could I. Be safe, little sister.*

I felt the welling of emotion from Aine. She wasn't the only one who felt it.

Then the blue dragon turned her amber eyes on me. *Soon we shall have lessons, Aodan. I am Zedhal, one of the teachers.*

I'm looking forward to it, I thought.

What else was I supposed to say?

A puff of smoke escaped from Zedhal's nostrils. *What else indeed, little brother? Go and kill the monster.*

We will, Fangorn thought. *Now we must go. Come Aine, Aodan.* He bent for a moment, letting his snout touch Voko. I could tell he said something, but he had his door shut.

A light flared between them, and then Fangorn stood up so quickly I wasn't sure I'd seen it.

I felt what I thought of as the dragon hum of Hell, yeah.

This was like that movie, Men in Black. Where the one guy kept saying, Hey, I want that flashy thingy. There were a shit ton of flashy thingys here.

You'll learn, Aine thought.

I hope so.

Fangorn moved away. It was amazing how graceful he was for such a large dragon. He ducked his head as he left the cavern.

Aine and I hurried after him.

How goes shifter practice? I thought.

I felt her huff of impatience.

I do not understand why I cannot shift! It's maddening!

Drake's probably glad. He'd never win an argument again after you learn how to shift.

She was quiet, and then I felt an elbow down around what would be my waist.

Thank you for your support, brother.

It will happen.

You had no struggle

I still struggle. It happens when I don't want it to. I walked in here and shifted without even thinking about it. I don't like that lack of control.

We both have it, but it manifests differently.

Another thing to practice, I thought.

I saw the flash of her teeth as she smiled briefly.

We can portal from here. Fangorn had stopped in front of us.

Faster than I could blink, he shifted.

Aodan, you need to shift.

What? Oh, shit, right. Hang on.

I closed my eyes and saw myself as human, completely clothed. I'd worn my coat today. Part of me wondered if the other dragons would be bothered, but Fangorn hadn't been, and I felt better when I wore it.

I looked down.

Nope. Still dragon. Sighing, I closed my eyes again, and thought about the details of my coat, and my boots.

I felt liquid for a moment, and then when I looked down again, my boots were there.

Nicely done, Aodan.

I wish I could do it faster, I thought.

It will come. Are we ready?

We both nodded.

He waved a hand, and the portal opened.

Where are we going? I thought.

Drake and Brennan are with Stefan in the Dragon Realm. We are going to them.

You think that guy will help us? I mean, I feel for him, if he was really framed for something Eilor did—but we don't have proof.

He's the best we've got right now, Aine answered me.

Fangorn had strode ahead of us, his pace determined and tinged with anger.

Aine watched him. "We will need to help him," she said.

"Why?"

"Because he is very angry. Voko is the oldest of us, and she is like a mother to all of them. If this is Eilor—"

"Who else would it be?"

"No one, but we have no proof. And we need proof to undo whatever magic has been set upon her."

"We can't just break the spell?"

"Magic is very personal here. If you wish to break a spell, you will need to have the caster break it or…"

"Or?"

"Break them."

I walked on a few steps in silence. "You sound like Fangorn," I said finally.

"The more I am with him, and the dragons, I feel the dragon within me. It's like it's been asleep my entire life."

"You know, Aine—"

My thought was cut off by Fangorn calling out to Drake and Brennan, who I could see standing in the distance outside of a small wood structure. It wasn't anywhere near as big or grand as the stone house I'd been in with Eilor.

Drake patted Fangorn on the shoulder and hurried past him to us. Well, to Aine.

"I am glad they gave you back." He took her in his arms, and she rested her forehead against his.

I moved on, feeling like I was intruding in their intimacy.

A hand grabbed my shoulder.

"I'm glad you're here, too. I know what it's like to be dragged into something that isn't your idea," Drake said to me.

Aine smiled at him, and he put his other arm around her shoulders as they caught up with me.

"Choice seems to be in short supply here," I said.

"Well, that happens when you're at war. And we are at war. We've been at war far longer than we thought. Aine and I have done well working to repair the damage he did to the people of this Realm, but he had a thousand years to make a mess of things."

"A mess?" I laughed. "That's an understatement!"

"How is she?" Drake asked as we came to where Brennan and Fangorn stood.

"She is holding strong against him, but the pull of the spell is strong," Fangorn said. "It is a spell, and it is draining her. While I do not care for guesses, the person who could manage to achieve this is Eilor. We must find him."

"Would that we found him right after his daughter died for Cian. We could have settled this then," Brennan said.

"Would you have killed him?" Fangorn asked.

I could tell he didn't believe that would have happened.

"Yes," Brennan said. "He harbored and nurtured those who would have killed us all."

Fangorn nodded. "What has he found?" His head indicated Stefan, who had come out of the door of the wood hut.

Looking at the hut, I thought my condemned apartment was bad. At least it had more than one room. This must be one of the desperation hideouts.

"He has not been here," Stefan said.

"Show us why you believe this," Fangorn moved quickly. "In the hut. Show me."

Brennan started to speak but stopped as Drake put a hand on his arm.

"It's good for him to have to prove it," he said quietly.

Brennan looked at Drake carefully, then nodded.

We waited in silence.

A silence which stretched on forever and was only broken by a shout and a roar from the hut.

I was running before I even thought, Aine on my heels. "Fangorn!" I shouted.

The little wooden house burst into flames.

16

"*A*ine, wait!" I shouted. She couldn't go in there. Not in her human—fae—form.

She said something, but I couldn't hear her. As I ran, I felt the shift. I almost hesitated with the fire and remembered, Nope. Can't get burned. I lowered my head as I ran into the door, and the wood shattered.

I didn't feel her next to me, which was good. This would be dangerous for her without the protective skin of a dragon.

"Fangorn!" I shouted again, and I could hear my dragon.

The smoke was gray and thick, but I saw a figure in the corner.

Help me with him, Fangorn said.

I moved to the figure, and it was Fangorn. He hadn't shifted, and he held a slumped Stefan.

What happened?

We were looking through papers and bottles, and the explosion occurred.

So a trap, I thought.

A trap. Can you carry him? It will be easier for you.

I bent down and picked up Stefan. Well, shit. What do I do

with him? I don't have shoulders like I think about as a man—I ended up cradling him in my arms.

Like a grumpy, sneaky baby.

The image made me grin.

Take him out. I'm going to see if there's anything worth salvaging.

Won't the smoke—

No. Take him out, Aodan.

I pivoted, managing not to fall on my face or ass. The dragon thing was getting a little easier, thank God.

I ducked to not hit the door as I walked out with Stefan. For myself, I didn't care, but I might catch hell if he got hurt on my way out.

Are you all right? Aine was next to me. *Is he dead?*

Yes, and I don't think so.

I felt her hand on my arm, and then Brennan and Drake were heading toward us.

"Is he alive? What happened?" Brennan asked.

"Where should I put him?"

Drake moved next to Aine. Some kind of communication passed between them. If I hadn't been looking at her, I would have missed it. Then Drake nodded, and the moment passed.

Brennan turned to Drake. "Call Taranath and tell him we need his healing skills."

Drake nodded and pulled out a mirror.

I remembered what Brennan had said before we went to rescue Margrite. That having a more instant communication form would be helpful. As it was, they had our equivalent of cell phones. But I spoke with the dragons faster and easier.

Focus, I told myself.

"Fangorn said that they were looking through paper and bottles, and the explosion just happened."

"So while Eilor may not have been here, he made sure that his work here was protected. Damn that man," Brennan crossed his arms, glaring in the distance.

"Yeah, a trap."

"He's good at that. What happened to Stefan?" Aine asked.

I shrugged. "I don't know. All I have is what Fangorn told me, what I told all of you."

"Where is Fangorn? Do you need to go back and help him?"

I smiled. "No, we are fine in smoke and fire. I think he wanted to see if there was anything useful left."

"Here I thought having dragons around would be a chore," Brennan said, the hint of a grin tilting up the corner of his mouth.

"What, you mean we don't enhance everything?"

"I would have said no, but I am finding that I am wrong. Which, as my wife would tell you, occurs more than I realized."

I laughed at that. Iris sounded like Margrite.

I hoped that Margrite was okay. A pang of guilt at leaving her washed over me.

She is fine, Aine thought. *She wanted you to be with us.*

How do you know?

Dragon talk, remember? We can see what's going on with her.

I didn't see it.

She snorted. *You need to get out of your own head more.*

Drake returned. "He'll be here momentarily. He's not going to die before that, will he?"

We all looked down at the man I still held.

"Perhaps not. He's breathing."

"Well, I suppose that's good," Drake said.

Stefan coughed, and stirred.

At that moment, I saw a flash of light, and then Taranath was walking toward us.

"Is he still alive?" He asked without preamble.

"Yes," I answered.

"Well, if you would please set him down, I can examine him. Was he directly in front of the blast?"

Aine, Drake, and Brennan stepped back. Did they think I would explode?

Maybe, Aine thought.

Shut up.

"You'll have to ask Fangorn," I said.

"Should you go and check on him?" Drake asked, eying the flames.

They were getting higher, and I could feel the increased heat on my back. I lay Stefan down, trying to be gentle. I wasn't sure if I succeeded, and then I stepped back.

Okay. Be a human again. I visualized myself as me, closing my eyes.

I didn't feel the shift. I peeked out of one eye, and nope. Still dragon. Okay.

Inhaling deeply, I focused on my own face, and this time, I could feel the shift.

When I opened my eyes, I was me again. The first thing I saw was the red leather of my coat.

"How do you do that?" Drake's voice broke my internal focus.

"What?"

"Shift, change," he said.

I noted that Aine was listening intently, and remembered that she hadn't been able to shift, which clearly pissed her off. She hid it well with just expressing frustration. I imagined she kicked the shit out of things when no one was looking.

Her eyebrow went up. I hadn't meant for her to hear that.

Drake, along with Brennan and Taranath were staring at me with great interest.

It felt … weird.

"I don't know, really."

"How do you keep your clothing intact?" Taranath asked.

"Well, um … the shifting to my dragon is easier. Sometimes, I don't even think about it. It happens with the situation."

"Like this one? You shifted as you ran to the hut?"

The heat on my back grew more intense, and I looked over my shoulder to see if Fangorn was on his way out.

You alive in there? I thought.

I am. I am almost done looking through what I can. Is Stefan alive?
Yes, but I'm getting the third degree here. Be great if you could join me.
I shall be out shortly.

Was he laughing at me? It felt like it.

Thanks, I thought sourly.

The noise I could hear was definitely a laugh.

Fine, burn, I thought.

Aine turned her head away.

"Um, yeah, I didn't think about it then."

"Did you know you wouldn't be burned?" Brennan would be a good interrogator.

"Yes. I … well, when I first shifted, I tried burning myself."

Silence, and then Drake laughed. "Completely understandable, Aodan."

"Drake operates that way for many things," Brennan said.

"He's fearless, which makes everyone else worry," Aine added.

Thankfully, the banter eased Brennan's gaze as he regarded his brother. Which was good because it meant he wasn't laser focused on me.

"So that is how you discovered you were immune to flames? What else did you discover?"

Shit, the gaze was back to me.

"I don't know. That wasn't my best moment," I said.

"I should very much like to speak with you more about this," Taranath said from where he knelt on the ground next to Stefan. "Later, perhaps."

"Yes, it would be wonderful if the healer focused on his patient." Stefan had come around at some point.

"You're awake," Drake said with no great amount of pleasure.

17

*W*e all looked down at Stefan.

"You needn't sound so disappointed," Stefan answered. He gingerly felt along his face. "Am I bleeding? It feels like my face was hit."

"No, you're not. I gather you were close to the explosion, but you don't seem to have sustained damage."

"The dragon pushed me aside," Stefan said.

I wasn't imagining the reluctance in his tone.

At that moment, Fangorn appeared. He carried a sheaf of parchment in his hand, a bundle of rolled papers. His face was streaked with ash, but otherwise, he looked unharmed.

"Stefan is right. Eilor has not been there recently. I could find no scent of foods, or drink. I did find these," he held out the parchment.

Brennan took them but didn't unroll them. "What are they?"

"Spells. As best as I can tell, and I did not have the time to be thorough, he was experimenting with altering spells of the blood."

"What is it with this guy and blood?"

"He wants to be a dragon. He wants to be like the two of you," Stefan said.

"What?" Drake said.

But all four of us looked at him.

"That doesn't surprise me," Aine said.

"I told you of his response to seeing a dragon punish a fae man. It stuck with him. For years after that, he would say that if someone could be like a dragon, no one would offer them any trouble." Stefan pushed himself into a sitting position. "Thank you, mage. I am sorry, I do not know your name. But I am fine. And thank you," he looked at me. "You carried me out."

"I am Taranath, and you're welcome," Taranath said. "I have not heard the story of a fae man being punished?" He looked up at Brennan as he stood.

Brennan sighed. "My grandsire, named Corwen, was most … fierce. He would sentence fae who killed other fae, or harmed children, to punishment by dragon."

"So civilized," Fangorn said.

You could have cut steel with the knife in his voice.

"He was, in some respects. In others, he was fairly primitive."

"It was he who consigned us to Eilor's care."

"He did. I cannot make that right. What I can do is change the future," Brennan said.

I felt Fangorn relax. That was weird.

"You are doing your best, Goblin King. I apologize for allowing my temper to speak for me."

"If you've never seen a man killed by dragon, it's something you don't forget," Stefan said.

I was glad he brought the conversation back on topic. The focus on shit a thousand years old was mystifying for me. Nor did it solve the problem at hand, which was where was Eilor and how did we save Voko?

"I agree," Fangorn said.

Stefan looked surprised to hear agreement from one of the dragons.

"Killing in battle is different than killing an unarmed being in front of you."

Did you? I thought before I could stop myself.

No. But I watched it.

His tone did not invite discussion, even in my head.

"All right, what does this tell us about Eilor?" I asked.

"That he has not been here, and that he is working with magic—or trying to work with magic—that he doesn't understand fully. It's speculation."

"How can you test that?" Taranath wondered.

"On my children," Fangorn answered.

Well. Another conversation killer.

"And how do we know he hasn't been here?"

"The notes are dated, and they are over a year old."

"He's very precise when making notes on things he tries," Aine said. Her arms were crossed, and she had what I'd call a weird expression on her face.

You okay? I asked.

Drake saw it too. He put his arm around her.

"I would like to have these notes back for our own studies," Fangorn said to Brennan.

"Of course," Brennan said. "May I ask that Taranath and his apprentices be allowed to copy them? I shall return them to you as soon as that is done."

"Yes. I am concerned at Eilor's insistence on our blood, specifically Aodan's blood, right now. I would like our spell caster to study these."

"I would very much like to spend some time with him or her," Taranath said. He turned to Aine. "Did he take your blood like this?"

He had a very open and frank manner that allowed him to say this, even in what could be called a tense conversation.

Fangorn stared hard at the mage. Taranath didn't look bothered by this. He must be the only person, like … ever.

"I would be willing to speak with our caster, and see if he is willing," Fangorn said finally.

"No," Aine said. "Only a few times. I guess it wasn't what he was seeking."

Although her tone was neutral, I knew she was bothered.

You're still dragon, I thought.

Why can I not shift? Her response was super fast.

I don't know. We're all different? Why can't I control my shift? Why does it happen when I don't even realize?

These are all questions for our caster, Fangorn interrupted.

I thought back to earlier. That would be Ynos, the tall orangish dragon.

Tarnanth nodded. I wondered if he could feel the shifts between the three of us.

The three dragons. For the first time, I saw myself as something more than just that guy trying to make it, trying not to get killed.

Well, I was still trying not to get killed.

"What is our next stop?" Drake asked. "Much as I like burning down any place for Eilor to take refuge in, we still haven't found him. And I see no proof that you know how," he added, turning to Stefan.

Stefan sighed, looking bored. "I can only move as fast as our party moves, Dragon King."

I looked down to hide a smile. The egos of everyone but me, Aine, and Taranath were enough to build a suit of armor with. No one here took any shit from anyone else.

They are all strong, Fangorn said. *It's not a bad thing. This is merely establishing the….*

Pecking order? I asked.

I am not sure. What is pecking order?

How chickens establish who's the boss.

Fangorn actually snorted. Everyone looked at him, and he waved a hand as he coughed. To cover it, I guess.

What are chickens? Why do they peck?

Small birds that lay eggs. We eat the eggs and the chickens.

You'll need to show me these.

You'll probably be offended, I thought.

"None of you can help yourselves, can you?" Drake glared between Fangorn and I.

"What? Did I miss something?" I'd been paying attention.

He shook his head. "No, I recognize the signs of someone head yelling."

"Can Eilor still talk with dragons?" Stefan asked.

Fangorn did grin then, a toothy, I'm-about-to-eat-your-ass-sucker grin. "Not anymore. He has lost that ability."

Brennan held up his hands. "We will not inquire further, then. One less asset for Eilor is a good thing. Stefan, let us continue to the next place you listed. Taranath, you are free to return to the Castle."

Taranath nodded and sent a smile around to everyone before turning and opening a portal so fast that it seemed like…magic.

Duh. Magic I still didn't have control over. At least I hadn't tripped as my amazing blue dragon. I'd take the small positives where I could.

I sent up good vibes for Margrite. Other than when Eilor had kidnapped her, I'd never willingly been away from her.

You're taking this worse than she is, Aine remarked.

She can't turn dragon and fry someone's ass, I thought.

She is strong, stronger than you credit her with.

I sighed. *Probably.*

"Are you three done?" Drake had his hands on his hips. "Aodan, you were supposed to be an ally." In spite of his aggrieved tone, I could see the humor in his eyes.

"We are," Aine said smoothly. "I will go to Taranath and

oversee the copying of the parchment. It could help Voko," she added.

She touched Drake on the side of his face, and he lifted his hand to hers. Then she moved off, and like Taranath, she practically disappeared in a flash of light.

Hey, I want to be able to do that, I called to her.

We can't always get everything, brother.

Whatevs.

"How do they do that? Portal so fast?" I asked.

"Practice," Brennan said. "I cannot portal as fast."

"You always have a caravan in tow," Drake grinned. "I'm amazed you're alone."

Brennan smiled. "The baby is not having a good day."

"Just to catch me up," I said, holding up a hand. "What, exactly did we discover here?"

"Some moldy papers, and one of Eilor's bolt holes gone," Drake said. There was no humor in him anywhere.

"The papers may help us, and if not, our caster will continue to work," Fangorn said. "This is not going to happen in an instant."

"What about Voko?" I asked angrily. "She's—"

Be still, Fangorn growled at me.

Why?

We do not discuss our own among outsiders more than we must.

Oh, what happened to family? I asked. *That whole line you were feeding me before?*

We'd both moved closer together. I was livid at the ever-changing agenda, and the fact that Fangorn wasn't telling me everything.

What are you hiding, Grandfather?

hy do you think I am hiding anything? Fangorn sounded defiant.

A sure sign of hiding something.

"I am unsure what is going on, but I think we will leave you two to discuss this," Brennan said, as if there weren't sparks flying from both Fangorn and me.

He opened a portal and stepped through. Drake followed him. As I watched, I realized he, at least, had been telling me the truth. He did not portal as fast as Aine or Taranath. He looked like a turtle to their roadrunner.

The light winked out, and I came back to Fangorn.

"I'm not kidding. What the hell aren't you telling me?"

Speak among us, please. I do not want to take the risk of someone over-hearing.

I threw up my hands and marched away. *Who is going to hear shit? We're out here all alone, with a burning shack. Voko is dying, and what the hell are you doing for her? And why aren't you telling me the truth?*

Why would you say that, Aodan?

Like a wind whipping across my face, I could hear the rest

of the dragons listening in. They must have been trying to ignore us, give us privacy. That had abruptly shifted.

There was someone else … Margrite! I felt a spark of happiness that my best friend was here. It would make it easier if she could hear things in real time. I always forgot stuff when telling her later.

Then I returned my focus to Fangorn. *Why do I think you are not telling me everything? Do you want me to list the reasons?*

Yes.

Oh. Shit. *Okay, I will. First, you got me back here the first time on false pretenses.*

What do you imply? His voice took on a dangerous tone.

But I was tired of the bullshit, and not in the mood to dance around him and his dangerous tone.

It was convenient as hell that Margrite was kidnapped. You wanted me back here, and that made it easy, didn't it?

Are you suggesting that I somehow orchestrated it?

No. I am not.

I saw his shoulders relax.

But you were willing to use it to your ends, weren't you?

Wouldn't you, Aodan? You wanted to save your friends. I am trying to save all of us!

What the hell does that mean? Why do we need to be saved?

The silence that rolled through the collective after my question was deafening.

What? I looked at Fangorn. *What are you guys not sharing? Time for no more bullshit, no more lies, or evasion.*

Aodan … Aine put in.

No! I know that you have to be all secretive, and paranoid, but all of us, me, the rest of them, Aine, even Margrite—we're friends. Family. I'm not going to hurt you, or anyone else. I'm here, aren't I? For shit's sake, Fangorn!

I threw up my hands and stomped away from him. This was trying to find info and no one wanted to talk.

Where are you going?

Footsteps followed me.

Hell if I know. I don't even know where I am. But I'm so pissed. You're not telling me the truth. You haven't told Aine the truth. She gives you a shit ton of leeway, but I don't operate like that.

How do you operate?

I stopped and turned to face him. *I am a thief. That's how I've made my living. It's how Margrite and I survived. I'm not ashamed of it. I stole shit. But one thing I never did was go into a job blind. If the person hiring me didn't give me all the details, that was it. Deposit forfeit, and you can hire some other schmuck.*

Schmuck isn't a good thing? His eyebrows were up, and his arms were crossed.

No. It's being played for a fool, and I'm nobody's fool. Not for you, or anyone else. So it's time to give me all the details, or I'm done.

I crossed my arms and glared back. My eyebrows stayed level. He was a lot more drama llama than I was.

Fangorn held my gaze, and then he sighed and looked down.

I'd won.

Although I probably ought to hold off on the victory dance. For the moment. It was coming, though. I could feel it.

It's time, Fangorn, I heard from far away.

His head shot up. *I am not sure, Voko. And you should not be speaking. Conserve your strength.*

I am sure. It is time. If we do not tell them, and something happens, perhaps like what is happening right now, how will they go on? How will they do what they need to for themselves, for any of us still here?

Fangorn shook his head. I could feel the conflict coming off him.

Do you really want to keep this to yourself forever? I asked.

It is how I have kept all of us safe. Our silence has allowed all of us to live.

Eilor cannot harm you anymore.

Really? His head came up. *Voko might disagree with you.*

And look what's happening! The fae, your former enemies, are trying to help you, help her. You're not alone or locked in a dungeon anymore!

I added that last bit because from one of the dragons I could see the cavern I'd seen before, the one that had cages and bad lighting.

Fangorn's eyes glowed very bright green. *You shouldn't speak of what you don't know, Aodan.*

"How can I know anything when you won't tell me anything?" I yelled. "If you want my help, you need to tell me what it is I'm helping with."

He walked away from me.

No! Don't walk away! Aren't you tired of carrying this all by yourself? That's why you want my help, Aine's help, right? Because you need it, and because carrying this shit is killing you.

That is not what is killing me, his voice was soft.

Then what is?

We are killing ourselves, Aodan, came another voice.

I wasn't sure who it was. It wasn't Voko. I thought it was one of the female dragons.

Fangorn, Aodan, Aine, Voko said. *Come home. Come home, and we will share.*

But, I am—Aine began.

She's right, Daughter, Fangorn said. *Come home. We must all be together.*

He looked back at me. *Come, Aodan. You're right. It's time.*

Then he opened a portal and walked through.

Shit. Even when all mad and unsettled, the old man's portals looked pretty spiffy. I really needed to practice this, I thought as I followed him. You know, when life threatening shit wasn't happening all around me.

My eyes adjusted to the dark of the Caverns. My soul ... I inhaled deeply and found that I'd shifted.

Wait for Aine, Fangorn said.

I stopped, and in less time than it took me to blink, she was stepping through a light that was gone as fast as it had appeared.

"You gotta teach me how to be all fast like you," I said.

"You have to teach me how to shift," she grumbled.

"Done."

She smiled up at me. Then a frown passed over her face. "I hope this goes like you want it to."

"Stop worrying. The truth, even if it sucks, is always better when you're heading into something hard. I don't want to be surprised anymore."

Aine didn't respond, and we both followed Fangorn, who'd walked ahead without speaking.

I recognized where we were headed. The chamber room where Voko was. It was if I could feel her. As expected we turned through a door on the right.

Voko was curled into a ball, looking all the world like a big, gold cat. With bigger teeth. Fangorn shifted and walked to her, bending his snout to her head. She inhaled deeply as he did so, and I felt the other dragons, who were spread out along the edges of the room, sigh.

Whatever he'd done, it made her feel better.

I thought that Ynos was the spell guy. Huh.

Leaning down, I whispered to Aine, "How do you feel right now?"

"Almost at peace," she answered.

"Me, too. You want to try to shift?"

"What are you talking about?" She looked mad.

"All the dragon fu all over the place here? This is the time. Let it go, Aine. You're wound so tight that if I poked you hard, you might explode."

"I have no idea what you just said," she said primly.

"I'm saying I can feel your tension, and I think you might be in your own way, because not shifting pisses you off every time you want to shift and can't."

Aine crossed her arms. Was it a family trait? She and Fangorn looked pissed off the same way. Which meant I probably looked the same.

All pouty? I heard from Margrite. *Yeah.*

Shut it, I thought.

"Seriously, just stop worrying. It's going to happen. Let yourself feel this place."

Wise words from the youngest, Voko said.

Fangorn stood next to Voko, and the other dragons moved closer.

He looked around, and then started to speak. *You see before you, Daughter and Son of my son, all that remains of the dragons of the Dragon Realm. We are of many clans—*

Firebringer.

Devourer.

Pyremakers.

Hearthspirit.

Nightflame.

Lastblaze.

Ash.

Heartglow.

The voices chimed in. I could hear the pride and the ache in all of them.

Those are not the only clans, but the ones that are left. We were not like those of our clans. We did not see the point in fighting the rest of the Fae Realm in all out war. Yes, we are dragons. Yes, we can lay waste with a single breath. And yes, our magic is fiercer than the rest of the Realms.

But there were more of them, all the Realms working together. And we lost.

The only reason we were allowed to live was that ... Fangorn stopped.

You must tell it all, one of the males said.

Then I must go back before the Dragon War. Back to what we were, once.

I am so confused, I thought.

I am the only shifter left from that time. While I shift easily now, by the time the Dragon War began, none of us shifted easily, if at all.

Wait. Wait. I shook my head, trying to process what I'd just heard.

None of you shifted easily? Aine asked.

No. We'd largely lost the ability, or, in all honesty, the desire to shift. We didn't have to, outside of a few instances.

All of you are shifters?

We were once, a green male—Chevym—said. *We all have to shift.*

Why? Aine was better at this than I was.

My head was still spinning.

Because if we do not shift, we cannot reproduce.

y mouth fell open. I could feel it, and knew that once again, I was not the sexy blue dragon I aspired to.

I caught Aine's expression next to me.

"That's what he wanted, wasn't it?" She breathed.

I felt something shift within all the dragons in the room. I couldn't identify what it was, but this was strong. And not necessarily positive.

Yes, Fangorn said finally. *Eilor knew. He discovered it through the process of our surrender. He had help. A dragon named Tarlock—*

The cavern reverberated with the hissing of all the other dragons.

Holy shit.

Sided with the fae, with Eilor in particular, and told him. Told him that we were shifters, who rarely did it, but had to do so in order to mate.

What happens if you are not fae when you mate? Aine asked.

The child does not survive. Sometimes the mother does not, either. That was the orange female, Ymri.

Why didn't you shift anymore?

As time went on, we were less included in the decisions of the Fae

Realm. We were some of the strongest casters and practitioners of magic, and yet the fae, and the trolls, dwarves, and goblins all backed away from us.

By the time Jharak's father, Cathair, who was the Fae King, was on the throne, we eyed each other with great suspicion and distrust. They did not trust the strength of all that we could do, nor our shifting ability. We once had wolf shifters within the Fae Realm and the fae enslaved them. The idea of shifting was seen as something less than.

I could hear the scorn in Fangorn's voice.

Every dragon child was taught to shift, of course, because we had to. But most of us preferred to stay in dragon form. It feels better, right. And why would we want to be like those that smiled to our faces, and tried to subjugate us when not looking into our eyes?

That makes sense, I thought. I had to say something.

Well, you would think so, but in reality, we were hurting no one other than ourselves. We ensured that we were more and more separate. Which is not the case. We are fae, but we are fae shifters. We look like other fae when we are not dragons. To create a greater divide brought us to where we are now, with only thirteen of us left. And a madman hunting us, wanting our blood, wanting to be one of us.

The dragons hissed again.

Surely not? A green female came close.

So says the brother of Eilor.

Why? She asked.

He saw a punishment, Imi, Fangorn thought. *I find it weak, but his brother says the scorching stuck with him. He was properly afraid of us, and our power.*

He looked over to where Aine and I stood together. *That is why I suppose he wants your blood, Aodan. It's why he wanted to mate you with me, Aine.*

More hissing.

What? I turned to my sister.

Her face was a mix of misery and anger. *It's true.*

That sick bastard.

Yes. Her lips were a thin line.

At first, he wanted Ailla to mate with me, or another dragon. When he realized that so many of the women died, he decided he didn't want her to suffer that fate. But that was only after many of the women left in my cage did not survive birth.

A feeling of despair, and anger, and hate washed through me. I realized that I was feeling what Fangorn was feeling.

How many? I asked.

Thirty-one, he answered immediately. Of those children, only Lionel survived. His mother was a girl that Eilor found in one of the villages, an orphan.

No one would miss her, Aine thought.

The bitterness dripped from her.

Precisely. Her name was Ena, Fangorn continued. *And while she was the last of the women Eilor sacrificed to me, I loved her. I cared for all of them, but after the first few, I knew their fate.*

What happened to her? I asked.

She gave birth to Lionel, and then one morning, she and the child were gone. He'd come in and taken them both. I hope that she was returned to her village, but I know it to be only a wish. Eilor killed those who were no longer of use to him. She could have told someone what he was doing. No, she is gone, as is my son.

I felt the hum of the other dragons, and I knew they were offering the strength of all of us to Fangorn. His sadness and anger warred with one another, and I could feel it as though it were my own.

Why does he think he can be a dragon?

I do not know. It is not something that one can change. Either you are or are not. You must be born from a dragon to be a dragon. Merely having the blood of one will not suffice.

Does he have your blood? I asked.

He did. He obtained two drops of it and made the jewel that your friend now wears. He wanted to see if he could hear us. Tarlock told him of that, as well.

Did he tell Eilor everything?

Fangorn nodded. *And then he died at Eilor's hand.*

He burns a lot of bridges, I thought.

If you mean once he is done he discards the person he was using, yes, he does.

Okay. Then we need to stop him. Not only from running around making shit messy, but from getting near to one of us. How do you think he got to Voko?

I do not know. And that is worrisome. He has never been able to penetrate the Cavern of the Ancients. Not physically, and not via magic.

Um … I wanted to ask another question but didn't know how to ask.

Ask, Aodan.

Is mating with a fae woman the same as mating with a dragon? I braced myself for the laughter.

No, it is not. Being a dragon … changes … things as you know them. I assume you know the—

I waved a hand. *Yes. No need for details.*

God, just what I needed. The birds and the bees from Grandpa Dragon.

When two dragons mate, the child comes from an egg. But there were dragons who mated with fae who were not shifters, and that child was born fae. It didn't happen often, but there were a few.

That's weird, I said.

It is how things happen, Fangorn shrugged. *I felt certain, as Eilor forced me to attempt to create children, his tribe, he called them, that most of the children would not live. It takes a special fae to carry a shifter child to birth.*

Okay, so we know what he wants. He may or may not be the one hurting Voko.

It's him, Fangorn said.

Why hasn't he contacted you?

He cannot. He no longer has the means.

I shook my head. *I don't buy that. He's resourceful. He's not super smart, in spite of what you guys all think. I think he plans well, and he's cunning. That beats smart on a lot of days.*

Then what do you suggest?

I shrugged. Please, please please let my dragon 'whatevs' look as good as I'd seen it on the other dragons. *I don't know. I need to think about it.*

We do not have a lot of time. Putting aside everything else, the amount of energy we—and Voko—are using to keep her well is great.

"When do we ever have a lot of time?" I muttered.

I felt an elbow from Aine.

What do you think? I directed my thought at her.

He didn't leave many notes in his journals. I found three of them, and I've poured over them. Wherever he kept the notes about what he did with Fangorn, I haven't been able to find them.

That sucks, I thought.

There is more, Fangorn said.

The other dragons weren't expecting this. They'd known the story he was going to tell us. But this, whatever it was—this was new to them, too.

I believe the cure is in the papers we found with the Goblin and Dragon Kings. I have kept that paper back. After we eat, and rest, we will see if this could be a possible cure.

Why didn't you say anything? I thought.

The talk of the other dragons muted out my question. Everyone was speaking at once. I stayed quiet, and waited for the talk to die down.

You should have told us this immediately, Fangorn, Ymri said.

He sighed. *It involves more than just me. It's both a spell, and an item.*

What was he talking about?

Fangorn continued. *The papers talked about breaking all manner of curses, spells—any sort of magic. It referenced the Ancestors' Stone.*

That is merely a tale to tell children, Gramuss said.

I don't believe so. Eilor followed all those children's tales. He notes that he has the stone, hidden somewhere. I went all over the hut where the papers were found. It was not there. In order to heal Voko, we must find the stone. Then we use the stone to cast the spell. The Ancestors Stone is capable of healing all magic.

Surely you don't believe that, Ynos said.

While I do not care for Eilor, he has found more of our history than any other. These were based on his finding notes from Markan.

There was silence, and then Ynos spoke again. *Do you believe it could be from Markan?*

Who's Markan? I thought.

The first of us. He was the one who petitioned the Fae King to establish the Dragon Realm. He trained the young dragons at that time. Brought them out of hiding.

How do you hide a dragon?

That is a good question. We do not know, Gramuss replied.

Eilor believed he had the Ancestors Stone. We must find it. It will be in one of these hiding places. We will need to be there every time one is discovered and searched.

I could feel the rest of the dragons around me, their minds humming with thoughts.

Aodan, when the stone is found, you will need to steal it.

What? I'm retired!

There is no other way. If the fae kings know what this is, they will never give it to us. And if we do not have it, Voko will die.

Dammit. I didn't want to steal anymore. Particularly from Brennan, or Drake, who I liked.

We must see to our own survival, Fangorn said.

Aine? What do you think? I was hoping for an ally here.

I don't know, she said.

Let us eat, and then retire, Fangorn said.

That was kind of abrupt.

We will go and procure food, the light blue dragon whose name I couldn't remember stepped forward. *Fangorn, will you rest here with Voko? I would like to go out for a bit.*

Of course, Zedhal, he answered her.

She moved quickly to the door, the two green dragons following her.

I'll sit with Voko, if you all would like to go, Aine said.

I'll stay with you, I added. I thought they would be out flying, and while part of me wanted to go badly, I knew it was the right thing to stay with Aine.

How I knew, I had no idea.

I am too angry to sit still, Fangorn said. *Call for us if she—*

We will, I answered. I didn't want him to finish the sentence.

There was a lot of quiet thunder rumbling through the floor as the rest of the dragons moved out of the room. I could feel their excitement, their eagerness—their desire to be in the sky.

I was glad they were gone. I didn't want to think about stealing again. Get over yourself, I told myself. You steal. This will be easy. Then I pushed the thought from my mind.

Come, young ones. Sit, and take my thanks for staying with me, Voko thought.

We both moved to her, Aine sitting by her head. She put her hand on Voko's neck and leaned into her.

I didn't know where to put myself and fumbled around settling on the floor of the cavern. This whole four leg thing was awkward still. I didn't even know how to begin to curl up like Voko. I finally managed to lay on my stomach and get my legs and claws in a mostly-comfortable position under me.

Tell me of your shifting, Voko said to Aine.

20

*W*hat *shifting?* Aine sounded disgusted. *It's not something that has happened. Why?*

I kept quiet. Margrite often told me I was not always sensitive, but I figured that input from me would not be welcome.

Aine didn't answer.

Voko said, *I heard what Aodan said to you. I wonder if he might not have insight not considered.*

Oh, by the moon and stars! Aine got up. *He's not the savior of everything!* She moved away.

Shit.

I focused hard and managed to shift back to my human form before she came back to us.

"I am not the savior of shit. I'm here because I have to be, and part of me wants to be. That part is completely opposite of the part of me who wants to be in the Human Realm, in the life I worked my ass off to make with Margrite. She's my best friend. We've been together for nearly ten years. She has my back. I have hers. And I've left her, to who the hell knows what? So don't dump that shit on me. I am not saving anything, Aine."

I took a breath. "The only thing I do understand fully is that if you want something to work, the entire team has to be committed. It's why Margrite and I only worked together, and why I had one guy I worked for. Because a lot of people are crappy team members. If you think there's something I should or shouldn't be doing, I'd appreciate you sharing it. I'm not from here. I don't have the history you do. You know Fangorn. He's different with you than he is with me. You understand what we're up against here!" I threw up my hands. "All this history, people holding grudges and shit from a thousand years ago? It makes no sense to me. After this long, who cares? Eilor needs to die, and we need to find what we need for us. That's it. All the stuff with the fae—that's stupid to me."

Moving close, I looked at her, keeping eye contact. "But it's not stupid to the people here. I need help in knowing when to shut my mouth. You helped me with that when we were planning how to get Margrite back. I have no idea of what I'm stepping in sometimes."

She met my gaze steadily, not giving anything away. I could appreciate that.

"You need to figure out what's in your way, and stop whining," I finished.

Her eyes sparked. "Stop whining? How would you know what it's like? You know nothing, and you shift as easily as ... as ... sneezing!"

"Voko, anytime would be a great time to get in on this," I said. The dragon had been quiet since Aine and I started talking.

You two need to work things out. They are there, simmering. We can all feel it.

"Thanks," I said.

"What's so special about you? Why is Eilor after you? Why you?"

"And not you?" I asked. "Are you kidding?"

Aine turned away, but not before I saw the pain on her face. This wasn't about me. I walked to her, reaching out to put my hands on her shoulders.

"What is this? This isn't really about me," I said. I hoped like hell I was right, because she might kill me. She had all the magic-y stuff, and she was good at it. I didn't stand a chance.

Aine faced me, and her eyes were very bright, and shiny. Like shiny with tears. Her lips were pursed tightly, and her face … I looked down. There was a lot of pain there.

"It is, and it is not," she said.

"Well, that makes a metric ton of sense."

She came closer and gave me a hug. "You're supposed to be my sibling, the person I get to be close with. No conditions, no … no entanglements. But with you, I feel more entangled than with anyone. I feel like we are in a competition."

Wrapping my arms around her, I let my chin rest against the top of her head. "We're not. But I get what you're saying. I feel that way sometimes. I come up short a lot."

Aine leaned back. "How can you say that? You've managed being a dragon without any problems!"

"Whoa, sister, slow your roll. I have problems all the time. Just because they don't look like your problems doesn't mean they are non-existent."

She frowned. "But you can shift."

Women. I swear. I didn't understand them. We were right back where we started, except Aine and I had been shitty to each other.

This isn't the best way to get anywhere, dumb ass, I heard.

Thanks, Margrite.

I hadn't known she was still listening.

Always, she replied. *I can't turn any of you off. It's like a soap opera that runs twenty-four-seven.*

I snorted. *You okay?*

Why wouldn't I be? Stop being rude.

I felt a door close. That was interesting. But she was still there, even though she'd put up a door between us. It felt more like a privacy curtain.

I won't kill you, Aine said. *Tempting though it may be.*

That isn't how you foster trust and teamwork, I replied.

She smiled, a small, tentative smile. It was enough.

Let us speak, then, of your shifting. What have you been doing to practice? I know you have been. Voko chose this moment to come back to the conversation.

Aine visibly sagged. *I keep trying to see myself as a dragon, and I can't.*

What do you mean? I asked.

She sat down, close to Voko again. *I mean, I can't see myself as a dragon. I have seen all of the dragons here, and I try to see myself like them, in their colors, or height, and I can't. All I see is myself.*

The dragon and you are one, child, Voko said.

I watched the golden dragon. She was breathing steadily, but shallowly. I didn't like it. Her eyes were closed, and every so often, a small puff of smoke rose from her nostrils. It reminded me of the box job—the one where I crouched on a beam and tried not to cough myself to death.

Smoke had come out of my nostrils, then, too.

I have spent so much time here, with all of you. The ancestors are strong in this place, and I do not shift. Aodan and Fangorn shift the moment they set foot in the Caverns. But I do not.

I told you what I think, I thought. *You're thinking about this too hard. Let it go.*

That is very easy for you to say, Aine responded.

Sure, but I can't control it. I've told you that. I'm trying to hang onto the dragon, not let him get too out of control. You're so in control, there's no room for your dragon.

Aine burst into tears.

I hated it when women cried around me. Margrite was sure this had something to do with my mom, and after seeing the things I'd seen, I was inclined to agree with her. It made my upset, and uncomfortable, and twitchy as hell. I wanted to solve whatever problem that had brought on the crying.

Which is not always possible.

Aine got up and walked out of the room.

Holy sh—ah, crap, I thought to Voko. *What did I say? I wasn't trying to be a jerk, or anything. More like, thinking out loud.*

One of her eyes opened slowly and regarded me. *I think that you might have said something that was a truth to her.*

You think? You are so not helpful with the words of wisdom. Oh, God. Way to go, Aodan. Pick a fight with the sick dragon.

The corner of her mouth that I could see turned up. *It's not on me to give you words of wisdom. At best, I am there to lead you to them.*

Again, with the so helpful commentary.

Do you value that which is given, or that which you discover on your own?

I sighed. *All right, you have a point.*

The eye closed, although the mouth remained in an almost smile.

Your words are wise, however. There is nothing about a dragon that can be forced. Even when we were fae, we were stubborn and at times, unyielding. Looking back, we thought it meant strength. Now, I feel it might have been ... unwise.

You're kind of the master of the understatement, aren't you?

The mouth lifted further. *It is one of the prerogatives of age, young one.*

Should I go after her? I looked to the door. I couldn't hear Aine, and she'd been gone longer than it should have taken to cry a little and kick the nearest rock.

No. Leave her be. We can talk of your shifting. Why do you feel you cannot control your dragon?

Oh no, Grandma, you don't get to analyze me!

Her eye opened, and she huffed in what sounded like a laugh. *Good for those around you, but not you, eh?*

Damn right. I answered with no hesitation. *I've had plenty of head shrinking. No need for it now. Where is everyone else? Does it always take so long to get food? Can't you guys just go snatch up a sheep, or cow, and barbeque it?*

You really don't like to talk about yourself below the surface.

Good way to get killed, I thought.

Not here. When we can all hear one another, and we feel what others feel, it is good to sort out your inner turmoil.

No thanks.

You may refuse, but that will not be something you can do forever. After a time, others get tired of your turmoil.

What do you mean?

We are a collective. We know all of one another's secrets. While we do practice avoidance and allow for some privacy, for the most part, we know one another intimately. You are a bundle of secrets tied with twine of pain and anger. It is a burden for you. Consider how that will affect your dragon family.

Are you laying a guilt trip on me?

Is it causing you to reconsider some of the things you've said to me?

I hesitated, then, *Perhaps.*

Then yes, consider this a trip to guilt.

You're totally like a mom.

We all have our roles. You must learn to work with your dragon. Your fine speech about teamwork needs to be put into action within you.

Oh, totally a mom. Turning my own words against me.

The best kind, child. I don't even have to come up with them.

How are you feeling?

The same as I did some time again. Do not change the subject. You and your dragon are one. You must think and act as one. He is not separate from you. He is you. You are him. The dragon is an extension of you. From the manner in which you speak, you do not view things this way.

I started to reply, then stopped. *You're right. I don't see him as me.*

Why is that?

I sighed. *Because if I do, there is never any going back.*

There is no going back now. You are a dragon, Aodan, and no amount of wishing or denying will change that.

But … if I don't embrace all these things, I still have a choice.

You have a choice no matter what. Your father lived in the Human Realm for many years. He was happy. Had Eilor not found him and his mate, I do not think he would have returned. He knew the dangers.

How could he leave all this? I asked before I could stop myself.

I do not know. The relief and happiness I have from once more being in the Cavern of the Ancients is beyond description. It's our home. It's our heart. We draw strength from it. It must have been very lonely for your father.

I didn't say anything, and she continued.

But he was strong, and it is a testament to his strength that he fought for his family to the end. Like we all would. He embraced the dragon as part of himself, not a separate being.

You're saying I have to own all of me?

Indeed.

I considered this when a crash outside the door made us both look over. I stood, thought, I could use a little dragon strength right now, and shifted. Crouching, I stood in front of Voko, ready to kill the shit out of anything that wasn't supposed to be here.

More crashing, and I felt a growl rumbling deep in my throat.

Steady, Voko said. *Something is amiss, but I do not sense anything other than dragons.*

Anything else will die, I thought.

A shadow appeared in front of the door, and then I saw the long neck and head of a dragon.

I felt myself relax from my bunched position. *They're back,* I said. *About time. I'm starving.*

Food sounds good, Voko agreed. I—

Her words were drowned out as we both heard it

Help! I don't know what to do!

The dragon I'd seen in shadow fell into the doorway. It was about my height, and a mix of red and blue, a magenta color.

Help, the dragon said again.

Aine? I asked.

21

*O*f course it's me, Aine said. She didn't sound pleased.

You've shifted!

You are indeed in full grasp of the situation.

What happened?

She didn't reply.

I was right, wasn't I? I could feel a grin spreading across my face. I hoped it wasn't the I'm-about-to-eat-you grin. That one was kind of shitty.

No. Yes. Maybe. I don't know.

Well, get up. Let's see you, I said.

Another pause, and then, *I can't.*

I stared, and then started to laugh. *Yeah, shifting on the fly, even without control, it's so great, isn't it?*

You are not helping, brother.

That's not my job right this minute. Right this minute, as your brother, who was until recently your punching bag, it's my job to gloat and snicker.

Snicker?

Yes. Snicker. More than once, even.

When I can stand, I shall kill you.

I laughed louder, the deep boom of my dragon's voice echoing around the walls of the room.

Aine the dragon looked to Voko. *Can you not make him stop? When will I have more control?*

I caught the slight movement of Voko's shoulders. How did she do the dragon whatevs lying down? That was skill.

You need to be more in tune with your dragon fu, I said to Aine.

Please, Aodan. I heard every word of you and Voko speaking.

Yeah, well, I'm what happens when you and your dragon fu are not one. So learn from my screw up, sis.

She pushed out her front legs, and then carefully, got her back legs under her. *This is so odd!*

Stop thinking of them as hands.

Aodan may be your best guide, child. None of the rest of us were ever fae—or human—for as long as the two of you were. We were dragons before we could even remember. We learned how to manage as both from infancy.

Aine carefully pushed herself up, standing first on her hind legs, and then with a wobble, sitting back on them.

Steady? I asked.

Almost, she replied.

Take your time. There's no rush.

I am not sure I believe that, Aine said. The frustration in her tone showed in the straining muscles, and the fact that her jaw was locked shut.

Why would I lie to you? I asked. *Seriously, way to go. And take your time.*

What happened for you? Voko asked.

I do not know.

Welcome to my world, I said.

Not helpful, Aodan.

I'm all you got, I thought.

I am doomed, Aine thought.

Voko made a choking sound behind me. I sprang back to her.

Are you all right?

It is good to hear young ones, she thought.

I felt the warmth and happiness that radiated from her. How could she put out so much feeling when she was so ill?

I could die tomorrow, and that would not negate my happiness, Voko responded to my thought.

You're not going to die.

She sighed, the pale smoke rushing from her nostrils. *Everything dies, Aodan. Some merely live longer than others. Help your sister.*

Hesitating, I watched Voko for another moment.

I will bide, Aodan. Aine needs your help.

Aine was still sitting on her back legs in the doorway. I moved to her, feeling much happier that my own dragon fu was cooperating. For all Voko's words, I did not feel like the one driving the bus, here.

Okay, you need to figure out the four legs thing.

It was so funny to see Aine's facial expressions on the dragon face. She was not pleased with the prospect.

What, you've never fallen on your face before?

Not since I was little.

Well, get prepared. When I first shifted, I was all impressed with myself. Great color, loved the scales, and I was beautiful, blah blah blah. Then I took two steps and fell right on my face. On my nose, actually.

The hint of a smile cracked her stern visage. *Really?*

Yes. It was a lesson in not believing your own hype, I thought. Opening my memories, I let her see things from my eyes when I was first trying to navigate as a dragon in the warehouse.

She watched as the moment replayed itself. *Is that really how it happened?*

Why are you so worried?

I hate falling.

I sighed. *Remember what I said earlier? Let go of that shit. No one else can see you, and you and me are different. We didn't grow up both. We're having to learn it now, when we've been something else our entire lives. Cut yourself a little slack.*

All right. It's very strange, how this feels, yet doesn't feel, like my body.

I know. I didn't need to say anymore.

Slowly, she fell forward, landing onto her front feet. After a moment, her eyes met mine.

Start walking, I thought.

First, one foot. Then the other front foot. Then a back foot. She fell.

That looks a lot more graceful than I managed, I thought.

You might be right, Aine thought from the floor.

I like your color, I thought. *No one else here has that. Fangorn is blue, and our fa—dad was blue, as well. I wonder where the purple-y color came from.*

Is this musing good or bad? I can't tell, Aine thought as she pushed herself up again.

Neither. I'm kind of thinking out loud. Fangorn is a blue with green. You can see it in the light. But you and me, we're the blue that has red behind it. It's more red in you.

Are you fierce when angry? Voko asked.

Very. But I do not show that side to many.

Why not? I asked.

To show anger is to give over control.

I started to speak and remembered who had raised her. And how it mirrored, in some ways, my own childhood. You never let people know what was really going on. Because Aine was right. If you showed something real, that gave others the chance to use that, to control you.

We're more alike than you think, I thought.

Perhaps, Aine took a tentative step.

I have found that our fiercest were red and orange. Usually, bloodlines and clans determine the look of one. But I also suspect that temperament has something do to with it as well, Voko thought.

You've studied this? I asked.

No. But when you've seen as many of your own as I have, patterns emerge. Aine, close your eyes and walk.

So I fall even more?

So you stop trying to manage it, Voko responded quickly.

Aine huffed, but she closed her eyes. She took a few steps and stumbled. But she didn't go down. A few more and she paused, opening her eyes.

I hate being wrong, she thought.

Sucks, I agreed. *Keep walking.*

Did Eilor believe you could shift? Voko asked.

Aine's purple ridges over her eyes came down. It made her look serious and fierce. *I do not know. I always thought he was disappointed, because Lionel—father—shifted much earlier. But he also did not expose me to all of you like he did with Lionel.*

He learned his lesson with that child, Voko said.

It killed our dad, I corrected. *Who gives a shit what lesson Eilor learned?*

Child, your father was always someone who would die in Eilor's mind. I am thankful that he got away, that he was able to find a mate he loved, and that he had the joy of being a parent. When he was brought back to the Dragon Realm, he shared with Fangorn. He lived a happy life in the Human Realm.

While being hunted.

The dragon whatevs shoulder came into play. *Everything is hunted at some point. Even we were, and none of us ever thought that was possible. Lionel was able to choose what he wanted in life. Had he stayed here, that would not have been possible.*

She sighed. *I think there is some greater purpose in the two of you being here at the same time, learning your shifter side at the same time.*

Like what? I asked.

Aine was listening hard. *I think the others are back.*

Well, don't we have something good to show them, I grinned at her. *Almost better than dinner.*

A roar, the sound of many dragons, reverberated through the room where we were, and the entire cavern.

All three of us looked to the door.

That did not sound good.

22

"*W*ho enters here?" A voice roaring and full of menace, rose over the rest of the noise.

Kyldret, Voko thought. *One of our red dragons,* she added.

"It's us—Aine, Aodan, and Voko!" I shouted, letting my dragon voice roar a little. It felt good.

"Who else is with you? Do not lie—we know!"

What the hell? Fangorn, there's no one else here!

We know there is another dragon with you.

Are you kidding me? Yes, there's another dragon. Why don't you come and meet her?

Voko said, "I believe that you will be a good leader, Aodan."

"Why would you say that?" I hissed. It was hard as hell to whisper as a dragon. "I don't want to lead anything!"

The dragon whatevs shrug was my only answer. It wasn't looking as cool as it had been. Maybe because it was directed at me so often.

Thundering steps in the corridor and then Kyldret, the large red male, and Ynos filled the door. Fangorn stood between them.

"Where is this dragon?" Fangorn asked. His voice was icy and cold.

"Right here," I stepped back and threw a claw toward the back wall where Aine stood on all fours. I could feel her fear. She didn't move.

Fangorn stepped between Kyldret and Ynos, a look of wonder on his face. As with Aine, I could see the man within the dragon.

He stopped in front of her and placed his snout on her forehead. *It is you, my daughter.*

How could you miss that? I asked.

There has been no dragon that entered these Caverns without me in over one thousand years. It threw all of us off.

You didn't hear her?

I did not, and I apologize, Aine, Fangorn said to her. *I do not know why we did not. All I could sense was a dragon I did not know.*

He inhaled near her. *I know your scent now.*

You smell more … fragrant than I recall, Aine said. She hadn't moved from the wall.

Your sense of smell is going to make you crazy, I thought. I knew where she was going with this. As a dragon, you noticed that animals—which we were—smelled much more animal.

Aodan is correct. You will be able to smell more, and over greater distances than you did as a fae. How do you fare, daughter?

I fell, she admitted.

I believe that is normal, Fangorn thought, glancing at me.

Already addressed it.

Fangorn stood back. *Come in and let us meet the newest member of our clan,* he said.

One at a time, the dragons moved in. I was struck by their ease and grace. They were larger than I was, and they moved like dancers. God, I hoped I'd be able to move like that at some point. It was striking to watch.

Voko stirred. *Come stand with me, Aodan.*

I didn't understand her request, but I moved next to her left shoulder. I put my claw onto the top of her back. *How can I help?*

Welcoming is a strong emotion. I am weary. Having you close will allow me to lean on you, if you'll let me.

I didn't understand what that meant, but I'd do whatever she needed. *Yeah, of course.*

When it didn't seem the room could hold anymore, Fangorn spoke. *We have been fortunate to have the last of us here, as dragon, in the Caverns of our Ancients. Let her be welcomed by all, those here and those gone.*

Welcome, Aine.

The words echoed and hummed through the small room. I could feel the vibrations from the sound of all the dragons. But there was more—the walls themselves hummed. It was the ancients, the dragons who'd died.

They were here, too.

We are complete, Fangorn said. *The last of us is found.*

Found … found … found … echoed through the room. Through my bones.

From the ashes, we rise. After many years of slumber, and stagnation, we have new blood, new life. Those who have been lost are found, and those stolen returned. Fathers and mothers before me, welcome Aine, and her sibling, Aodan.

The humming died down, but it seemed like the cavern got darker. Then, from the top of the cavern, which I couldn't see, a light filtered down. It drifted lazily, not like a ray of sun or anything like that. It was made up of many smaller lights, moving and glowing, bumping lazily into one another.

Lower and lower it drifted and then the light split. Some of the moving bits went toward where Aine was leaning against the wall, and the rest came to me.

"What is this?" I asked Voko in a hiss.

Wait, and see. It will not harm you.

I straightened up, still keeping my claw on Voko. Being next to her calmed me, even though I thought I was supposed to be helping her.

The lights, which reminded me of a warmer yellow firefly, reached the top of my head. As they fell upon me, I was hit with memories, and information, and feelings, and so many things.

The force of all that came to me—into me? —made me stagger a little.

At the same time, I felt safe. Comforted. Part of something. The line from me didn't just go back to my mom and dad, and then to Fangorn, and his Ena, but farther back. I could see dragons In all shades of blue and green, some so light they nearly looked silver. And one who could only be called purple.

Let the clans welcome them.

There was strife, and conflict. Anger, and fire, and death. I could feel it. It was like the dream I'd had of the dragons fighting. But worse. Because I could smell it, hear it.

Feel it.

And the death. So much death. I'd smelled a lot of bad shit in my lifetime, but nothing smelled like this. It was overpowering, and it was heartbreaking. My kin were among the dead.

Then I saw him.

It was like a spotlight had been turned on. I could see Eilor on the battlefield.

But he wasn't on the field where others were fighting and dying for him. For the likes of him. He was off to the side, in trees. Watching, keeping himself safe.

A crash and a thud and then I saw the wing of a fallen dragon. It was green, and there were dark streaks running jaggedly down the wing I could see.

It was bleeding.

In my mind, I heard the dragon call for its brothers and sisters, for its clan. It was dying, and it knew it.

His name was Kirfan.

I could feel and hear the other dragons responding, but they were far away.

Eilor stepped out of the trees.

In his hands, he held a knife, and a vial.

Holy shit. Even back then, the sick bastard was draining dragons. Had he been trying to mix fae and dragon even then?

Kirfan, even though he knew that it was the end for him, glared at Eilor.

"You will die, fae."

"You will die first," Eilor said. He raised the knife, and then I felt the light of Kirfan wink out.

I shook my head.

Was I the only one who saw that?

No, we all did. But I had not seen that before, Ynos said. *We found Kirfan on the field. He chose to share this with you and Aine. There is a reason.*

He was Nightflame, Imi said. *As is Fangorn.*

And as are you both, Fangorn said.

While our clans are important, they have become less so as there are so few of us, Gramuss spoke. He was large, brown, and often silent. *We must put aside clan rivalries. But it is important to know where you have come from. And you are fortunate that one of the Ancestors chose to share his death with you.*

I need to sit down, I said, and I all but collapsed next to Voko. *I'm sorry,* I added. *I haven't been much help for you.*

You have, she answered.

How?

That does not matter. What matters is that you gave freely, and you have been welcomed.

I thought I was before.

Not like this. Not properly. We wanted you and Aine together, Fangorn said. *Speaking of which, you are lovely, my daughter. There has not been a dragon of your color in many years.*

I'm glad you like it, Aine said. She'd relaxed. *I am not sure I can shift back at this point.*

We will help you. If you cannot, then you may stay here.

Yeah, Drake might not be thrilled, I teased her.

You are fortunate, Aodan, that I cannot get up and kick you where it might be most instructive, Aine said.

The entire Cavern burst into dragon laughter.

Since I'm a dragon, too, I guess that's why I didn't go deaf.

It was the best feeling I'd had in a long time.

Laughter is the best way to welcome family, Kyldret said. *Now let us go and eat.*

Imi came close to where I sat with Voko.

Voko, can you come to eat? Or shall I bring you some?

Voko stirred, and then pushed up onto all fours. *I will join you.*

I got up, clambered is more like it, and I stepped back to let her move. I noticed that all the other dragons did the same. Fangorn followed her, and then the rest did as well. Aine and I were the last ones left in the room.

I think they are giving us the time to move slowly, she thought.

Good thing. That welcome knocked me on my ass.

It was very intense, she agreed.

You ever eat with them before?

Aine shook her head.

"You think they flame it before they serve it? Or is it still kicking and mooing, or whatever?"

"I don't know," she said aloud. "But there's only one way to know."

"God, I hope there's some pre-flaming going on. I hate blood."

I walked carefully next to her, and together, we headed out to see what it was dragons did when they ate.

The smell hit me before I saw anything alive or dead. There's no mistaking the smell of cooked meat.

Then I heard it. A bleating.

Oh shit.

In the corner of the larger room we'd moved to, there were heaps of … smoked meat. I couldn't get into more of it than that. They, whatever they were, were cooked.

But in the corner, behind a fence near the wall, were several pale things I thought might be sheep. Or goats. I didn't know. Something in the cow family, or barnyard hay-eating family. And they were alive.

We don't have to—

I don't think so, Aine responded before I even got my entire thought out. *I hope not.*

No, you do not, Zedhal, the light blue female, came alongside us. *You eat as it is comfortable for you. Some of us like the taste of burnt meat, some prefer to kill it ourselves.* She grinned, and in the dim light of the cavern, her teeth gleamed.

That's good. I don't know that I could manage to kill a ... whatever it was moving around in the corner. And then eat it.

You'll find your preference, Zedhal said. She moved away, heading for the pen.

"What a surprise, right?" I whispered.

"She's very…"

"Intense," I finished.

"Yes."

Well, let's eat, I thought.

We both headed for a burnt heap.

I sighed. A cheeseburger was the same thing, with a fancy food dress, I thought. Nothing different.

Something strange happened as I got close to the whatever-it-was.

My nostrils flared, and I could feel my stomach rumble. Boy did it rumble.

Before I knew it, I was taking a bite, and chewing a few times before swallowing. Then another bite, and another.

When I sat up, the animal in front of me was nearly gone.

What the hell?

I felt sleepy. The way you felt when you ate too much and were hovering on the edge of a food coma.

It is all right, Aine and Aodan. You may sleep in safety and peace, one of the dragons said. It was one of the guys, but I couldn't tell which one.

Leaning over, I felt myself slide to the ground. I'd worry about it later. Whatever it was. I closed my eyes, just for a moment.

23

My eyes flew open. There was a hum around me, a hum of conversation? I looked around, trying to place my location.

Rock walls, ceilings that went on forever...I was in the Caverns of the Ancients. I'd fallen asleep like the drunk uncle at Thanksgiving dinner after eating McCrispy the mystery barn animal.

Aodan, you are awake. Good.

Fangorn was near me, like a genie popping out of a bottle.

I think? I can't believe how much I ate, or how fast I fell asleep.

Being a dragon, after being human and fae only for so long, drains you.

Yeah. Like mad.

I'm glad you're awake, because we need to move.

Why? Are we under attack?

No, but we have things to do.

Where's Aine? Did she shift back? I looked down, noticing that I was human—fae—not dragon again.

Fangorn, who was also in fae form, smiled. *She shifted as she slept. I am sending her back to the Dragon Castle. Drake will be worried,* and they need to make arrangements for her if she shifts suddenly. She needs a place to be alone and be safe.

Is Drake all cool with that?

Fangorn might not have understood the slang, but he knew what I meant. *He has known of Aine's parentage for some time before they married. He knew that her shifting would happen. He's always believed it would. Aine, I think, had more doubt.*

Not anymore, Aine said.

That sounded like a grumble, I teased.

This … takes … some getting used to.

It gets easier. You want some help getting back?

Aine laughed, and I could hear her dragon behind her fae voice. The sound was deeper, throatier. *With what? Portaling?*

Ouch, I thought.

I am sorry, Aodan. I didn't want to miss out on the teasing. Thank you for your offer. I will be fine. I would prefer to tell my husband the latest on my dragon heritage on my own.

Probably better. Be careful, I said.

Why, I didn't know.

You as well. She walked to me and gave me a hug. *Thank you, brother, for all that you have done.*

You're welcome, I thought. I had so many remarks at the ready, but I kept them all to myself. She was sincere. I didn't want to be shitty about it.

A light winked, and then when it winked again, Aine was gone.

"When can we practice portals?" I said out loud. "Because she is so good at it, it makes me feel stupid."

Aine is a skilled caster, a voice said. It was Chevym, the green male who radiated calm. *Now that she has managed to find her dragon, she can focus more on her casting.*

I thought we had one.

There are never too many casters. Chevym moved toward the doorway. *Good luck to you both. And good hunting.*

What about Voko? I asked. In looking around, I didn't see her anywhere.

She is resting. She leaned to you and took some of your energy. She tells me that you allowed it. There was a question in the words.

Is that what she meant? Yeah, she asked. I said yes. She can have whatever she needs.

That is a great gift to offer another, Aodan.

She can't die, I said. *There's a lot I don't know, but I know that for sure. She can't.*

Fangorn clapped me on the shoulder. *You know the right things, son.*

The words pleased me, made me feel warmed inside. *Where are we going?*

We are meeting Brennan and Stefan. The Goblin King contacted me about somewhere they've located. Or rather, somewhere that Stefan took him.

You don't trust him, do you?

Do you?

Not a bit. He's kind of shady.

If his story is true, he was wronged by Eilor as much as any of us.

Yeah, but he needs to prove intent, don't you think? I looked over at him.

We are of the same mind.

He's been an asshole in my world for a long time.

Which suggests all is not as he says. I shall reserve judgement. The Goblin King may be more trusting, although I hope he has precautions in place we are merely unaware of.

Brennan seems awfully nice.

Fangorn heard the doubt. *He seems that way, yes. His queen has softened him with those he loves, and cares about. But the Goblin King in the Fae Realm maintains a great deal of responsibility. He balances the magic that flows through all the Realms.*

How?

I do not understand it. The last Goblin King was far too fond of Eilor, and things became ... unbalanced. So Brennan is cautious. Do not underes-

timate him. It is to your peril. He may present as a warrior as Drake does, but like Jharak, Brennan is skilled and resourceful.

Drake isn't?

Drake is very resourceful, and cunning. He is less … refined than his father or brother. He does not deal in anything other than honesty, and facts. That has made life for him in the Dragon Realm a bit more difficult, but he's found his place. He's a good leader.

Why aren't you the Dragon King?

We'd reached the place where we could fly out of the Caverns.

We're flying?

I thought you might like to. I enjoy flying over any other form of travel. We'll shift before we meet them.

Why don't you want them to see us as dragons?

Like Brennan, I am cautious as well.

I took a deep breath and focused on becoming the dragon me. This time, it worked on the first try. I opened my wings, stretching them. It felt good.

Ready? I heard Fangorn ask beside me.

Yes!

He opened his wings and shot upwards. The breeze from him hit me in the face.

One more thing I'd need to practice. We needed to get past all these crisis moments, so I could figure out how to be something other than the bumbling dragon.

But flying, once I made it out of the Caverns, equalized a lot of the bumbling I felt. I pushed off with my back legs, and swooped my wings down, propelling myself upward.

One, two, three, four … I concentrated on beating my wings steadily and continuously. Finally, I made it to the top where Fangorn perched, waiting.

Well done, he thought. *Let us enjoy the later afternoon, shall we?*

He turned, and leapt from the cliff, his wings opening and fluttering as he flew with the wind. I hadn't seen this when we'd flown the last time. It had been dark.

A dragon in flight was a beautiful thing. Even though I was sure Fangorn did this regularly now, I could feel the pleasure coming from him.

Aodan, do not tarry.

Here goes nothing, I thought, and I ran, as best as a dragon could, and tossed myself off the cliff. This felt scarier than it did when I couldn't see shit. This was a long way up, and that meant a long drop down.

One, two, three. Four, five, six. The counting kept me focused and kept me from looking down. Nine, ten, eleven.

Good, Aodan. Catch up with me.

Oh, great. I looked ahead, trying to see him. How the hell had he gotten so far away? All right, time for double time.

One-and-two-and-three-and-four, I counted, flapping my wings with each word, rather than just on the numbers. I felt my muscles bunch, and stretch, and realized how good the sun felt on my back.

Fangorn was getting larger as I got closer. I could see that he was drifting, like I'd seen birds do in the wind. He would go one way, and then the other, and the only thing I felt from him was a straight line of pleasure.

Allow yourself to use the wind. You will tire yourself otherwise.

I had to catch up with you.

And you have. Now let yourself relax.

As wonderful as this felt, the human side of me was kind of freaking out. The first time I'd flown, outside of my late night excursion before Margrite and I left the city, was rushed, and my overwhelming memory was contained panic. I inhaled, feeling the cool, crisp air move through my lungs. Stretched my wings out further, and then held them open, hoping like hell I didn't drop like a rock.

The wind puffed under my wings, and I felt it lift me, buffet me along. A small gust came to my side, and I veered in the opposite direction. I moved my wings—how I knew to, I don't know—and I was flying level, for the most part.

Oh my God. This was incredible. I wanted to close my eyes, to feel the wind on my face—but that would be certain doom. Instead I focused on Fangorn still ahead of me, flapping his wings lazily as he waited for me.

How are you?

Awesome. Fantastic. Scared to death.

You're doing well. Now follow me. He wheeled around to the left and soared away with only a couple of beats of his wings.

I did the counting again, so that I could make sure I was flying fast enough. This time, it didn't seem so tough.

Keeping my focus on Fangorn helped me to not worry about everything else. The wind smelled crisp, and cool. There was something different in the Dragon Realm than in the Human Realm. We soared over forests and thick trees—and it wasn't like the trees I'd grown up with.

The air smelled different in the sun, and then when the wind moved across my face.

It was similar, but different. Older? I didn't know what it was.

But I enjoyed it. I felt like I was part of the land itself.

And that was scary as hell.

Down here, I heard Fangorn.

He dived toward the ground, moving even faster.

I followed, but with caution. I wasn't sure of the landing.

Then I remembered we wouldn't be landing right where Brennan and Stefan were. Good. If I crashed and burned, I'd only have a small audience.

Fangorn headed for a small clearing in the trees. As I watched, he spread his winds out and circled, drifting slowly to the ground. As he landed, he took only a few steps before he shifted.

I can do this. I angled myself down, and felt the wind speeding up as I moved closer to the ground. Then I spread my wings, and it was like someone yanked me up by the back of my shirt. Ok, one more thing on the to do list.

The wind shuttled me to the right, then the left, and I got myself into more of a spiral by tilting my left wing down.

Fangorn watched without comment from below.

The ground came closer.

I stretched out my back legs, ready for impact.

Pull your wings in now!

Startled, I tucked in my wings, and I landed with a soft bump, rather than the jarring shock to my legs I was expecting.

Fangorn smiled. *That wasn't bad. Now you need to shift.*

Closing my eyes, I visualized me, and when I opened them, I'd done it.

"It's getting easier, yes?" Fangorn asked.

"A little. I still feel very clumsy. You guys slept for hundreds of years, and all of you are graceful. Thanks for the wing comment—I wouldn't have thought of that."

He smiled as he headed off to the trees. "That's what we're here for, Aodan. To help you. I am not the enemy."

I sighed heavily. "Sometimes if feels as everyone is the enemy."

He didn't respond, and I wondered if I'd gone too far. Then I decided it wasn't something to worry over. We had bigger fish to fry, as Tina had always said.

I wondered what she would think if she could see me now. If she could see me without screaming.

"They are just ahead. Do not mention that Aine has—"

"Okay. Anything else?"

"No. We must not appear too wary. That breeds suspicion."

This shit reminded me of all the reasons I'd worked only with Margrite, and then with Luke. Too much drama, too much of everything. People had to make things complicated.

It appeared that even in the Dragon Realm, things were the same.

24

The cottage rose out of the rock of the small hill it sat against. It was neat, tidy, and cleverly made. The roof was made of straw, or hay, or something like that, and it didn't look old or withered. It looked pretty good. The walls were stone. This reminded me of the place where I'd gone to meet Eilor to get Margrite.

He had a type of house that he liked. Well, maybe that was stretching it based on only seeing three of his bolt holes. But two of the three were similar.

Something to remember.

Fangorn pushed the door open and after a short pause, barely noticeable, he walked in.

I was right behind him.

But my spidey sense, or whatever it was for dragons, wasn't tingling.

We were in a short hall, and there were rooms to the left and right of us. There was a room at the end of the hall.

"Over here," Fangorn went right.

This was a study, or office, or something like that. Papers

were all over the floor, and along the far wall, bending over a table, were Brennan and Stefan.

Aodan, the Ancestors Stone is here.

What? Are you sure?

Can you not feel it?

I stopped, and let my dragon fu take over. There was something, something different. *There is something of us here,* I thought.

It's the stone.

You are sure?

Yes.

I couldn't remember the last time I'd felt nervous about a job, but I did now. Probably because I liked the guy I was about to steal from.

He may not have this thing on his person, I thought.

He will.

Yeah, well you're not the one who will get caught with your hand in the cookie jar, I thought.

What does that mean?

Never mind. I'll let you know if and when I need a diversion. What does this thing look like?

It is a crystal. Round and clear.

A crystal ball. I needed to steal a crystal ball. I hoped Margrite couldn't hear this. She'd laugh herself to tears. I tried to settle my nerves. I was glad we were doing something that would potentially help Voko, even if it meant I had to do something I didn't want to.

"What have you found?" Fangorn asked.

Brennan looked up, smiling, but his smile was strained, and tired. Probably Stefan. I found the guy a strain and tiring, and I'd barely spent any time around him.

"My dear brother has been here in the past month, I'd say. We found food in the cupboards, and evidence that he'd been making notes." Stefan waved his hand toward the piles of paper.

"Did he leave here in a hurry, or did you guys make the mess?"

"I think he might have left sooner than he wanted to," Stefan said.

"What information can we gather?" Fangorn, all business, asked.

"He is obsessed with getting your blood, Aodan. He mentions making you and Aine..." Brennan's mouth twisted. "Never mind, it's horrible. But he feels that a child ... of your lineage would give him what he wants."

"What, he's going to drink a kid's blood? You know, if you're right that he wants to be able to shift."

"All these years, and I thought he wanted to create a dragon army for himself. But all he was doing was working to find someone to make him a dragon? In all that time, he never asked me how one becomes a dragon in a way that made me think he wanted to be one," Fangorn said.

Stefan shrugged. "No is ever meant to know what he's doing. He's very secretive." He laughed, but there wasn't a lot of humor in it. "He thinks he is far smarter than anyone else."

"I knew that," I said. "I told you that. He's not. He's cunning, and a good planner. He plans for lots of eventualities."

"You did," Brennan said. He was frowning. Then his face cleared. "It's somehow less irritating to think he's a master of things."

"Well, yeah," I said.

God, this was the guy I had to steal from? Why couldn't it be Stefan?

Yes. Fangorn popped in.

Wasn't talking to you.

Thankfully, he didn't reply. I wasn't in the mood for conversation. We'd been doing a lot of that lately.

I watched Brennan with the eyes of a thief. Where would he hide it, the crystal ball? I swear, I couldn't get away from the woo woo shit no matter what I did.

As a dragon, I didn't think I was able to cast stones about woo woo anything, but that wouldn't stop me from complaining.

He had a pouch on a belt that hung on his right side. He wore pants, but they weren't jeans. They looked softer, looser. He was wearing a tunic that hung down, and the tunic was belted. Same belt that held the pouch. I couldn't tell if there were pockets, but everyone here seemed to use a pouch, rather than a pocket.

Going off behavior and what I'd seen, if he carried it, it would be in his pouch. I frowned. That would be a lot more difficult to pick.

Didn't most of the fae keep the magic stones in their pouches as well? I hadn't used on, but they looked round. Like, you know, a crystal ball. I didn't think I'd have a lot of time to be digging around. It had to be quick.

I'd have to steal the whole damn pouch. Which was more difficult because he had it attached to a belt.

I don't think it's going to be as easy as you think, I thought.

Why?

Tell you later. But there's a lot of steps, and a lot of risk. Why is it we're not just asking him to use this?

"Is something wrong?" Brennan asked.

"What? Oh, I was just thinking."

"Well, it's not pleasant to contemplate. But it's better to know what he's thinking, and planning, then not."

I must have missed something, but I wasn't going to get into it.

Brennan watched me for a moment more. Then he directed his attention back to Stefan. "See if there's something to carry all these papers in. Less chance of losing them."

"Yes, your majesty," Stefan said. He didn't look thrilled.

He moved off to the back of the house.

"Sounds like the two of you are getting along great," I said.

You need to tell me if you sense it on Brennan, or just somewhere in the house, I thought.

It's on him, Fangorn said immediately.

You sure?

I am sure.

Brennan frowned again. "Did you not tell me that he was in a position of power and influence in the Human Realm?"

"Yeah. He scared the shi—I mean, no one crossed him."

"That much is obvious. The role he is in is not to his liking, and it's rather wearing attempting to manage his…disappointment at his new circumstances."

"He wanted to come back here. He is lucky he's alive," Fangorn said.

"That's if the stories about him are true."

"You don't believe they are?" Brennan asked me.

I shrugged. "When he was confessing his sins to me and Margrite, he seemed sincere. And both of us have a low tolerance for bu—for lies. I mean, he had a good reason to lie, but it hasn't really helped him, has it?"

"No, it has not," Stefan came into the study holding a leather bag. "I believe this will work. This was not what I planned when I said I wished to return home. I'm not a fool, however, and I realize that a price must be paid, whether I am telling the truth or not."

Fangorn was the only one of us who didn't look even a little bit bothered about being caught talking about Stefan. "And if you lie, this is but a mere waiting game. You owe your very presence here to the fact that my grandson is kind, and the Goblin King tolerant."

"I am grateful to be allowed a chance to prove myself more than my reputation. That doesn't mean I enjoy it."

"I think Fangorn is telling you to suck it up, buttercup," I said cheerfully.

Stefan looked right at me. I could see why he scared the shit out of people. It was an intense gaze, almost like those of the dragons. Almost.

But I was used to being glared at by dragons by now, so his tough guy act was nothing.

"Until I hear you speak, I forget how much time I truly spent in the Human Realm."

What the hell? "Didn't think you'd be slumming that long?"

"I didn't think I'd live that long." With no further explanation, Stefan moved to the desk and began putting the papers into the leather bag.

Fangorn moved closer to Brennan and began to speak in a low tone. That gave me time to talk with Stefan.

"What do you mean?"

"What are you asking about?" He didn't look at me but continued stacking the parchment pieces neatly.

"Were you trying to die?"

"Is anyone ever so patently evil?"

"Um, yeah. Your brother."

"You could be right. I don't see him as evil as much as I see him as incredibly selfish and focused. It just looks evil."

"He doesn't give a shit about anyone," I shot back.

"He never did. It's how I ended up in the Human Realm."

"You mean because he gave you up?"

Stefan stopped with his stacking and gave me the oh-so-intense gaze again. "Yes. The most selfish person I've ever met had a conscience at one time, and graciously handed over his own brother for justice. I thought you grew up on the streets, Aodan!"

"I did. It's a pretty weak story."

He carefully placed the pile into the bag. "It is. Any half-assed cop could poke holes in it, much less anyone with a brain. But the fever pitch to root out those who had done wrong, to cleanse the Realms of those less than, was strong at the time."

"What are you saying?"

"I'm saying you haven't lived very long, Aodan. And that there's always a back story, some hidden info. You know that."

"Fair enough. What does that have to do with me?"

"Probably nothing. I am not your concern. I'm here at the pleasure of the Fae King, and I am well aware of the..." he swung the bag, now stuffed, over his shoulder, "Fragility of that pleasure."

It was interesting and more than a little unnerving to hear that the fae weren't universally regarded as the good guys. All the undertones from Stefan, and the definitive statements from Fangorn, suggested otherwise.

"You don't think things can change in a thousand years?" I asked as he walked by me toward the door.

"I don't think they change here as much as you'd think," he tossed the words over his shoulder. "We have all the documents, Brennan. I'm ready when you are."

Brennan nodded. "Let me finish speaking with Fangorn, and then we'll take these back to Taranath. Perhaps he'll be able to make sense of them."

Stefan gave a short nod and walked out of the house. I watched him, and then walked to the small window at the front of the study. He stood out in the clearing, hands on his hips. Throwing his head back, he inhaled deeply. I could see his chest rise.

He'd been telling me something, but it wasn't anything I didn't know. He'd already said that he was framed, that it was a weak story. That there was more.

But what? And why did it matter now?

This was why I kept my relationships to a minimum. I didn't like being involved in all this … stuff. And this—this was ridiculous. Some of this stuff had been going on for years.

I heard Brennan and Fangorn come out of the door.

Now would be a good time to get the crystal, Fangorn said.

Don't tell me how to do my job.

Then do it, please.

It's not as easy as you think, I thought as I moved closer to Brennan. I kept my eye on his pouch. The trick would be to accidentally bump him and knock it off. Then hand it back and palm the crystal before I did so.

But could I? This was a lot of job for a short amount of time.

What the hell? Of course, I could. I could...

My eyes widened as it came to me. Inhaling, I thought about my dragon. Big, too big for this room, gorgeous blue in color and—

I shifted and let myself stumble all over my feet.

"Oh, shit!" I yelled.

As I fell on top of the Goblin King, I sincerely hoped I didn't kill him. My dragon felt like it had fallen on the ground, not on top of a person.

25

"Oh, dear," I heard Stefan say from outside the house. "I hope he's not dead." He didn't sound all that worried.

Figures. Stefan reminded me of someone who watched little kids trip in front of him with a smirk on his face. Even if he wasn't as bad as his brother.

"Aodan! What happened?" Fangorn was beside me, taking one of my front legs and pulling me up.

"I don't know. I felt the shift coming, and I couldn't stop it. Is Brennan all right?"

"I … will live," I heard from under me.

As I got up, I palmed the crystal in my hand, and focused on returning to Aodan, the man. I shifted before I even got through the entire thought. I hadn't ripped his pouch from his belt, by some miracle, so I didn't even have to pretend to hand it back. No awkwardness at all. At least, not until he went looking for it.

Stefan watched as Fangorn helped Brennan off.

"I'm really sorry," I said, trying to look sheepish.

Brennan inhaled deeply, like someone who'd just sprinted like hell. "I am not damaged. Beyond my pride, perhaps," he added with a smile.

I felt like an asshole. He was so gracious, and I was stealing from him. I'd wanted to give up this stealing thing, despite the fact it was a skill. I didn't want to need it to live anymore, but that didn't seem to be in the cards right now.

Sliding my hand into my pocket, I let the crystal rest and my hand relax. This felt like crap. Stealing from someone I liked and respected sucked.

It is necessary, Fangorn said.

Get bent, I replied.

Voko will live.

You hope.

He didn't respond, and I let the conversation go. It was easier to wallow in my own misery at having to steal again.

Just because I was good at it didn't mean I wanted to keep it up. The whole goal of my master plan with Margrite was to get out of the life of crime.

A life she was leading without me. Speaking of which…

Hey, you all right?

I'm great. I take it you're not?

Her voice warmed me. She sounded happier, happier than I'd heard her in a long time. Weird that I could hear all this in my head, but I could. It struck me at times at how weird it was, but those times were getting less and less.

Not so much.

Aodan is chafing at things that have to be done, Fangorn cut in.

I'm having to steal, I said.

Well, not like it's hard or anything, Margrite said.

I don't want to talk about it. What are you doing?

I'm working, believe it or not. I have a job, working in the tourist infor- mation center.

All your ID worked?

As much as we paid, it should have, her tone was drier than before.

True. But you never know.

No, you don't. However, since I show up on time, don't have a demanding significant other or kids, I'm a prime candidate. The laughter was back.

You sound good.

I am good. I wish you were.

"Aodan? Are you all right?" Brennan's voice broke into my thoughts.

"Yeah, sorry. I'm good. I was just trying to figure out what caused the shift. The question is, are you all right?"

Brennan smiled. "I am. I'll have Taranath make sure when I return. If you hear from Iris, I'm sorry."

I knew how protective his wife was of him. "I'll manage. Sorry again."

He waved, and he and Stefan headed away from where I still stood with Fangorn. A portal opened, and they disappeared.

"You have to show me how to be more efficient with the whole portal business," I said, watching the light disappear.

"No time like the present," Fangorn handed me a stone. "You have it safe?"

I knew he was referring to the crystal. "I do."

"Then keep it so and let us return to the Cavern. Use the stone, and focus on the main room past the entrance."

Hey! Did I lose you? Margrite was still listening.

Sorry, in the middle of something.

Oh, so you took time out of your busy day to complain?

Yes, I did. I couldn't help but smile a little myself. *But only a little.*

I get off work in a couple of hours if you want to whine some more.

I may take you up on that.

Get back to work then and let me do the same. I don't want to get fired. First honest job I've had in … like ever.

Later, I thought.

I felt her move away. I missed her. But she sounded happy, and I was glad for that.

"I always knew she would be," Fangorn said. "Now concentrate."

I glared at him for a moment, then, closing my eyes, took the stone and pictured the large room he was talking about. I could see it as though I was there. I heard a small hiss, and when I opened my eyes, a dark blue circle of light was growing in front of us.

"Very good," Fangorn said.

As we waited, it got large enough for us to step into. He moved ahead of me.

"Once you're through, picture the light going dark. It will blink out quickly."

I could feel my dragon wake up as we moved into the Cavern. I wanted to fly, I wanted to be out, and away from all the concerns of these fae, these people.

Pulling the crystal from my pocket, I held it out to Fangorn. "Take this. I need to get out of here for a while."

He turned, and his brow was creased as he frowned at me. "You don't know this Realm."

"Then give me a babysitter. But I need to get out of here."

Fangorn regarded me in silence. *Kyldret*, I heard him call out. *Yes?*

Are you able to accompany Aodan? He wishes to fly, and I don't want him getting lost.

Of course.

Nothing more as we stood, and then I heard the heavy step of Kyldret.

I would be pleased to fly with you, Aodan, he said.

He did sound pleased. It didn't sound forced at all.

Thank you, I responded. I feel like I need to get out of here for a while.

So you have no goal in mind?

Nope, I thought.

He grinned, all his teeth gleaming in the low light of the cavern. *Then let us go.* He moved to the place where the cavern opened up, and sprang up, his wings sending a strong breeze as he moved up the toward the exit.

Don't worry, Fangorn thought. *Just go and fly*. Then he turned and walked away, shifting as he did so.

I let myself shift, and walked toward the opening shaft. I'd only done this a few times, and I was nervous still.

Come, Aodan! It is nearly evening, which is the best time to be out! Kyldret called down.

Taking a deep breath, I spread my wings, and flapped, feeling awkward. I rose from the ground, and then flapped my wings again, harder this time. I moved upward a lot faster than I thought. A few more beats of my wings, each one feeling smoother and more natural, and I popped out of the exit at the top of the mountain that the Cavern of the Ancients was in.

Kyldret was right. The air smelled like evening—there was a leftover hint of the sun, but the cool of dusk overrode it. It felt refreshing.

Finally. I was wondering if I needed to offer aid, Kyldret said.

I still feel more human than dragon, I thought. *But at the same time, my dragon wants to be out all the time.*

You are not yet one, are you? He asked.

I don't think so, no.

Once you are, you and your dragon will work together. You see your dragon as separate, and it's part of you.

Voko said the same thing.

She is wise. She is also correct. His wings beat lazily, almost effortlessly.

Right now, I'd like to not focus on anything other than kicking rocks, I thought.

What does that mean?

Oh, uh, nothing. I need to fly to let off some anger.

Oh, well, that I understand. Let us go. Concentrate on how you feel in the wind. Do not think on anything else.

For the next hour, that's what we did. We flew, and I followed Kyldret as he did barrel rolls, and diving and turning. It was wonderful.

It also allowed me to not think about being a thief in this

world. The one thing I didn't want, the one thing I wanted to leave behind.

While I was flying, I was just Aodan, a dragon, enjoying the night sky.

I think we should go back, Kyldret said.

Is something wrong?

No. But there is something. Let us go. He beat his wings hard, and shot away from me.

I followed.

We flew into the opening at the top of the cavern, and I practiced floating down. It was both weird and peaceful.

About twenty feet from the bottom, I remembered to pull in my wings, and I landed on the floor with a small thump.

What has happened? Kyldret asked.

26

*G*ramuss came forward. *Fangorn offered the stone to Voko. Then he spoke the words that Eilor wrote. It was …* He stopped.

I didn't think I'd seen a dragon at a loss for words.

Will you show us? Kyldret asked.

Gramuss held out a claw to each of us, and we both took them.

I was pulled into the smaller chamber where Voko had returned after eating. Her light seemed dimmer, although that made no sense. But it did. She was fading.

Fangorn strode in carrying the crystal I'd stolen, and he was lit like a dozen candles on a dark night. It made the dimness of Voko even more stark by comparison. He knelt next to her, and tucked the stone into her claw.

The stone glowed like a star, surrounded by her soft darkness.

Then Fangorn began to speak, in the language I didn't recognize. The crystal glowed even more brightly, lighting first Voko, and then the chamber around her.

Gramuss must have looked up, because my view shifted toward the ceiling, and I could see small lights moving above. They drifted down, settling all over Voko.

The crystal intensified, and I could see the other dragons shielding their eyes.

Fangorn's voice rose, and the light grew brighter, until it burst and there was nothing but light.

Then all was dark.

Voko? Fangorn said.

I am here, she replied, and her voice was strong and sure.

Gradually, the ability to see returned. Voko stood, the crystal in hand. *This is the Ancestors Stone*, she said.

The vision faded, and Gramuss released my claw.

Oh my God.

The three of us stood silently. I wondered if they were having a hard time getting their heads around what we'd all just seen.

Can we see her? I asked.

Come, Gramuss turned.

We made our way to the room where we'd eaten. Voko was there, and unlike the memory Gramuss had shared, she was bright, back to the way I'd seen her when we first met. She was healed.

She saw me before anyone else. *Thank you, Aodan, for bringing the stone. It is the Ancestors Stone, and it has healed me. When it burst over me, I felt as though the webs of the magic weighing on me were blown away.*

We're sure it was Eilor? I asked.

There is no other who could do it, or would want to, Fangorn said.

We have to find him, I said.

Indeed we do, Ymri said. *He cannot be allowed to continue to make trouble as he has been.*

First we need to let Brennan know what we've found, I said, directing my thoughts at Fangorn.

Why?

Because secrecy got us here in the first place.

Many things brought us here. We cannot let him know we have it. There is more to this Ancestors Stone than the healing of all magic harm.

Oh yeah? Like what?

It identifies dragons.

I shook my head. *What?*

It will allow us to see whether a fae is also a dragon.

How? What? Why? These seemed the pertinent things to ask.

Markan created this stone. If you place the blood of a fae upon it, their dragon side will show. Eilor discovered this.

Is this why he wanted my blood?

Yes.

Could he tell who was and wasn't a dragon?

No, Chevym said. *He would have to be a dragon to read our magic. He is not. So he not only needs the blood of a dragon, he must have the eyes of a dragon as well.*

Holy. Shit. My mind felt like it had just blown up a little.

So not only is it the woo woo healing stone, it can tell us who else could be a dragon?

It will allow us to find mates, to rebuild our people. There was a light shining from Fangorn I'd never seen before.

Fangorn, you're looking a little like the guy who got everything he ever wanted, and it's kind of scary, I thought.

I have. I didn't think it possible, but there's a way. It's not just up to us anymore, Aodan. There could be more of us.

What if there are no more of us? What if the gene or whatever died out in the fae?

We don't know. But we can find out.

What, call the fae in the Dragon Realm to the Caverns and ask them to hold out a finger while you just take a little blood?

He waved a claw. *There are problems to be overcome. But we have a chance at life now, Aodan. This is what you stole for. For the lives of your people.*

His fervor made me uneasy. *I think we need to come up with a plan that doesn't start a second war. The Fae Realm doesn't even know we're still alive, do they?* I was remembering something I'd heard Aine say.

They will now, Fangorn said. *We have found our lost ones, we have found the stone of our ancestors, and we will no longer hide in the shadows.*

Why did that make all my spidey senses tingle?

Fangorn swept past me, holding the stone in one claw. I wanted to stop him, but I really had no reason to do so. Something didn't feel right.

We'd won. We'd succeeded in saving Voko, but … something was off.

This isn't right, I said to Voko.

Then we will have to be the balance that makes it so, she replied.

I hoped that would be enough. It would need to be.

I watched the other dragons follow Fangorn until it was only Voko and I. I met her golden eyes, feeling some of the peace that radiated off her when she was not ill.

What do we do? I asked.

It is time you learn about being a dragon.

Can I learn to use a sword?

She laughed. *I believe that might be possible. Let us go to the older halls, and call your sister. I will teach you, and we will watch and see what comes of the Ancestors Stone.*

Voko's optimism crept through me. I hoped it would be enough. I followed her from the chamber, hoping like I'd never hoped before.

Then I squared my shoulders. It would be enough. It would have to be. Voko was right about one thing. We had to keep the balance. I could do that. I'd been doing it my whole life.

Only now, I had my dragon fu. And soon, a sword.

It would be enough.

End of Dragon Found
Book Two of The Dragon Thief

Want to see where it all began for Aodan? Click the picture, or use this link:
https://dl.bookfunnel.com/lw4j12jbcv

ACKNOWLEDGMENTS

This book, as mentioned in the beginning, is dedicated to my own personal Dragons. Everyone should have dragons on their side in life. I'm lucky in that I have more than one.

All my Dragons are driven, supportive, enthusiastic, and *there*. Like Aodan, I found my Dragons when I really needed all those things. Although unlike Aodan, they didn't crash land on me. But they are there all the same, and I love all of them for it.

Alex, Lori, Stephanie, Corinne, Bernadette, Andre, Shawn, and Nathan - you have my special thanks.

To all my readers, who offer suggestions, ask questions, and are part of this process, thank you.
Hearing from you is a joy.

I am a lucky woman to be able to do something I love. Which means my final and greatest appreciation is to my family. My husband and darling children who understand what it means when I am sitting at my computer, headphones on, lost in the screen.

ABOUT THE AUTHOR

Lisa Manifold is a USA Today Bestselling Author of fantasy, paranormal, and romance stories. She moved to Colorado as an adult and has no plans of living anywhere else. She is a consummate reader, often running late because "Just one more page!" Lisa writes the things she does because she really, really wants to live in a world where these kinds of stories happen.

She is a fan of all things Con, and has an entire room devoted to the costumes created for Cons. She served on the board of Rocky Mountain Fiction Writers for four years, and in 2016, was named the 2016-2017 RMFW Independent Writer of the Year.

Lisa is the author of the fae paranormal romance series The Realm, the Grimm fairy tale retelling Sisters of the Curse series, the Djinn Everlasting series which follows a free-lance djinn, the Aumahnee Prophecy urban fantasy series written with Corinne O'Flynn, and the urban fantasy series The Dragon Thief.

She lives as close to the mountains as possible with her husband, children and four attentive dogs.

Connect with Lisa online:
www.lisamanifold.com
Lisa@lisamanifold.com

Lisa Manifold
PARANORMAL | ROMANCE | FANTASY
Fiction With Flair

WRITTEN BY LISA MANIFOLD

Dragon Thief

Dragon Lost

Dragon Found

The Realm Series

Heart of the Goblin King

To Wed the Goblin King

Realms of the Goblin King

Rise of the Dragon King

The Companion Tales, Volume I

The Companion Tales, Volume II

The Aumahnee Prophecy

with Corinne O'Flynn

Eamonn's Tale

Marigold's Tale

Watchers of the Veil

Defenders of the Veil (2018)

Tales From The Veil

Stories in the world of the Aumahnee

with Corinne O'Flynn

The Portal Keepers

The Gimcrackers

Djinn Everlasting

Three Wishes

Forgotten Wishes

Hidden Wishes

Sisters of the Curse

Thea's Tale

One Night at the Ball

Casimir's Journey

Do you like being in the loop? Sign up for Lisa's newsletter! Shenanigans, book recs, and the latest news abound!

www.ingramcontent.com/pod-product-compliance
Lightning Source LLC
Chambersburg PA
CBHW022142240626
47153CB00007B/2471